I0647141

# A METHODIST IN
# A MONASTERY

Copyright © 2017 by Billy D. Haddock. All rights reserved. Printed in the United States of America. No part of this book may be used or reproduced in any manner whatsoever without written permission except in the case of brief quotations embodied in critical articles and reviews. Revised 2nd Edition

ISBN-10 0-9669608-3-1

ISBN-13 **978-0-9669608-3-9**

A Methodist in a monastery | Billy D. Haddock

# DEDICATION

Dedicated to my friend, Bill Armstrong, retired pastor and district superintendent of the United Methodist Church, Texas Conference.

# Table of contents

1 WHY?............................................ 3

2 SETTLING IN........................... 20

3 GETTING BETTER
ACQUAINTED ........................... 49

4 STORMING &
SURRENDERING ...................... 81

5 SATURATION........................ 102

6 RE-ENTRY............................. 130

7 A MONK IN THE WORLD.. 142

The following story is centered on a fictional psychotherapist, Will McKinney, who spins a story with just enough reality included that the story could be biographical … except for a subtle twist of psychopathology.

In the words that follow, Dr. McKinney tells a personal story that seems too far-fetched to be contrived.

*photography by the author*

# 1 why?

It's the third day of a new year. I started early this morning, so I can make it to my New Mexico destination in time for the first meeting of the class. Spiritual Direction school. A monastery. This is where I am headed as I drive down I-40 West toward Albuquerque. The terrain has been level since I passed Abilene, Texas. As I approach Santa Rosa, New Mexico, I feel the excitement rising as I see the mountains looming in the north. The Route 66 signs stir up nostalgia as memories of the past flash across my mind. Looking for the turn north just outside of town, I gladly exit the interstate and begin my ascent upward.

This monastery and the spiritual direction program offered had intrigued me for some time. As I have wrestled with the decision to attend, costing 4 weeks of my life and a few thousand bucks, I leaned on my modus operandi: Justify the commitment of resources. From an economic perspective, I worked the idea around until it made good sense. I told myself the reason for going to a monastery was to learn skills in spiritual direction (helping people grow closer to God). It would be useful and allow me to transition smoothly as I moved toward eventual retirement from an active counseling practice. So in my search for different schools and courses of study, I had arrived at this choice.

I also chose to go to a monastery for the some of the usual reasons that monasteries exist: to seek a refuge from an active, busy life and to immerse myself in an environment where I where I might do a better job of finding God.  In addition, I was seeking answers to a specific question that had been forming in my mind: How could I learn to live more from the soul, the essence of who God created me to be, and less from the false persona I had created to survive in this world?  I felt a yearning for 'realness' that I had been experiencing as scarce in our culture. I felt myself placing a value on authenticity and craving simplicity.

I traveled to the monastery expecting solitude, peace, quiet, and time for reflection and relaxation.  What was waiting for me, however, was an opportunity to deeply enter the practice of accepting and loving other people. Lessons in grace were waiting for me because the Benedictines accept all visitors as if they were Christ himself (a chief mission of this monastery).

You know people often say, in reflecting on the past, 'if only I knew then what I know now." This part of me, my Monday morning quarterback, I call my 'future enlightened Self.' This Self (aspect of myself) would show me complexity, instead of simplicity, fear, instead of peace, and warring entities, instead of spiritual refuge.

Although I was aware that people have callings to do spiritual direction, I didn't experience a true sense of that within myself. This was more like an experiment I was conducting, very possibly undergirded with some pride and hypocrisy that proved to be blind spots. I was convinced that I had all the experience I needed, given that I am a 'professional.'

Yes, I was dedicated to helping people to live and love better. I wanted to go deeper in my understanding of how to help nurture others in their faith and life journey. What I really wanted, though, just for this short four weeks was to escape from the problems of the world.

Officially, in applying for admission to the school, I wrote, "I had felt a leading and interest in spiritual gifts since my initial spiritual rebirth some 20 years ago. Over that time, I have read, taught, and counseled people, engaged in spiritual practices, and sought assistance through informal relationships. Now seems to be the time to do this." The application asked questions about my experience in church ministry, my present occupation, and Charismatic Renewal. The latter slipped by me without much thought as I referred to other answers for that section. Educational background, prayer life, and spiritual journey, no problem. These were easy to complete. I was even able to describe my experience with journaling and dream interpretation, much to my satisfaction. Yes, I felt a bit of pride swell up to think that I had been doing my homework and was quite prepared. To add to the egoism of the process, they even requested a recent picture, which I was happy to provide. There were other questions that slipped by me on the application which were more foreboding than I realized at the time: Ever been involved in the New Age movement or the occult? If yes, explain. I left those areas blank.

In discerning a calling, it never occurred to me to leave out the "I" in my thought process. I had a blind spot in considering what God's will was in the matter. I asked the wrong questions, such as, "Am I called to minister in this manner?" I would have been better off had I asked the right question from the beginning, "To what ministry am I called?"

I was on the symbolic road to Nineveh, asking the wrong questions and ignoring God. Unlike Jonah, I wasn't rebelling against God, just following my own agenda and seeking God in my own passive-aggressive manner. Like Jonah, I was anxious and afraid of what His calling would be. Either way, I was going west thinking I had taken the safest direction, not knowing how risky or dangerous it was.

Like many in the world, I contributed to my own difficulties and had come to understand how the following situations derailed me from my goals:

- Getting distracted through TV, movies, Internet, and wasting precious time;
- Getting stressed by getting out of balance in my daily routine and wasting energy; and
- Neglecting to discipline myself and falling away

from exercise, study time, and monitoring my ego.

I reflected on these things as I traveled in my brown Chevy truck to the monastery. The first of the year is a time of reflection, planning, and rethinking how I want to spend my life. The 11-hour trip gave me plenty of time for this.

## *"Why now?"*

Since I had felt the call to go deeper in my understanding of God's will for about 3 years, a school of spiritual direction was attractive to me. I also felt the need for a longer stretch of personal rest and renewal. The rhythm of long weekend breaks I was taking each quarter coupled with a week- long vacation each year wasn't leaving me renewed as in earlier years. The daily grind of doing therapy was wearing me down. " It's time to lengthen the break," I told myself.

In retrospect, I would have benefited from more discernment to consider my motivations for the desire to participate in this sort of program. Yes, I had fulfilled the requirement to participate in spiritual direction before coming to the school. It was required. However, spiritual director and I were so focused on my other interests, I didn't delve deeply into my true motivations. Like many other decisions in life, I didn't ask the right questions. My spiritual director didn't either." What questions?" you might ask.

Questions like, "Am I open to surrendering to the message of the entire Bible telling me who God is and how God is?" Like many, I had created a God of my imagination that was egocentric. Another helpful question I could have considered, "Do I believe God expects me to grow from the experiences I encounter?" I was so focused on getting away to relax and recharge my battery that growth was a fleeting thought at best. Yes, I had been exposed to spiritual direction, but so much of my journey had been solitary. "Do I really believe another person can help me in my spiritual growth?" "Is it possible that I can help another person in his or her spiritual growth?" The scriptures would have answered these and other questions had I looked more closely. However, I didn't even know to ask the right questions, let alone seek answers to them.

The hypocrite in me gave lip service to the Bible as a living, God inspired, document that speaks to us in contemporary society. I justified my lack of time spent 'in the word' by reasoning that the archaic language of the Bible made it too difficult to understand. I used scripture more as a research citation when wanting to justify my position.

You see, I trusted my reasoning. I was a responsible person, especially with therapy clients. In my opinion, spiritual direction was a reasonable adjunct to aid in one's faith journey. I never considered if I walked the walk enough to pass as a spiritual director. I could look back on my life and see a calling taking shape, especially to minister to the suffering and the desperate souls of this world. Yes, I was good at giving direction to people, making order out of disorder, and encouraging others. Some would say this was just playing God. "Was I?"

I had a few relationships in which the deepest things of the soul were shared. It was rare for me, though, to experience this depth. I had longed for the glow or countenance that naturally attracts people. I wanted others, even complete strangers, to perceive me as spiritual and ready to listen. On the contrary, I had developed a force field that protected me from others who might steal my energy or rob me of my sense of safety and security. There was no peace of spirit or soul in such encounters. I found that I was more troubled and hungry for love than able to give out an abundance of love. For me, at this point of my life, this was a core truth.

There is another question only my future self could ask: "Why did I feel the need to 'go somewhere' instead of searching for God in the fabric of my daily life?" A part of me was aware of the 'geographical cure,' that occurs within the addiction process, an attempt to sidestep the inevitable by moving away from one's playmates and play places. I could apply this wisdom to others, but not to myself. It was only my future Self who has now evolved who can apply this Augustinian view to my faith journey: "It's not by change of place that we come nearer to Him who is in every place, but by the cultivation of pure desires and virtuous habits."

A final question that went unasked and unanswered as I traveled toward the mountains of New Mexico where the monastery was located: "Will, are you ready to abandon some worldly indulgences to do this work?"

## *The Setting*

The monastery is situated in a mountain valley among the Sangre de Cristo Mountains at an elevation of about 7,000 feet with the Pecos River running through the property. It was rich in history, as I would learn later. I was looking forward to getting away from the current problems of the world, enjoying nature through long hikes and taking leisurely naps. I hoped to learn new ways of helping people that the retreat workshop promised. I was open to receiving some individual consultation, instead of being on the giving side, for a change.

As I drove north from I-40 on highway 84 to the intersection on Interstate 25 and took the Glorieta exit, I had to do a bit of finagling to find the road to Pecos. Through the backwoods on a winding country road, I finally approached Pecos in what looked like a valley. I would later learn that what is now the village of Pecos and the Pecos River Canyon has been settled since at least the 8$^{th}$ century. Ruins and archeological history are preserved at the Pecos National Historical Park just a few miles from the Abbey. Centuries before the arrival of the Spanish, native nomads and traders built a multi-story pueblo on what is now Glorieta Creek. In the 1400s Pecos Pueblo was a regional power and center of trade for the people of what is now the New Mexican plains.

History reports that the Coronado expedition passed through the Pecos area in September of 1540, which led to Spain claiming the area as theirs in the early 1800s. As we know in Texas, the area became independent of Spain and part of Mexico in 1821.

Texas fought for and gained their independence from Mexico in 1836. Seven generations ago, my great grandfather (you count the number of greats) fought in the Campaign of Bexar in November 1835 that resulted in the Alamo being taken from the Mexicans. In March the next year, the Texans were defeated by Santa Anna's army, which became known in Texas history as the battle of the Alamo. It was my dad's mother's people who settled in Texas before it won independence from Mexico or became a republic.

It would be 1846, after Texas became a state that the United States declared war against Mexico. On August 19th, 1846, New Mexico was claimed as United States Territory. The property on which the monastery is now located was purchased by Alejandro Valle on May 31, 1852. During the Civil War, the battle of Glorieta Pass was fought nearby. It was that decisive battle that thwarted Confederate efforts to break the Union hold west of the Rocky Mountains. The property was sold at auction to the Valley Ranching Company on April 10th, 1886, several years before the State of New Mexico joined the union. The Terrero Mine in the Pecos Canyon employed as many as 600 people from the late 1800s to mid-1930s. Ore was conveyed from the mine to the milling site just over the monastery's west ridge by suspended cable. Many of the roads and bridges in the area were built in the 1930s by the Civilian Conservation Corps.

The colorful history really added to my attraction to this place. My next challenge was to find the way up to the monastery. A stop at a service station yielded the directions and a fountain coke. I was good to go feeling the anticipation increase. I took a right turn leaving the store and I found myself driving upward toward the mountains. After what seemed less than a mile, I found a sign marking the entrance to the monastery just beside the gift shop. The road beside the gift shop led me down to a parking lot behind the hill and near the main building.

I later came to know that the gift shop had once served as a stagecoach stop along the Santa Fe Trail and as a post office for the mine. The carpenter shop down the hill and to the left, behind the gift shop, had been the stable. During the height of dude ranch popularity, the Valley

Ranch was a popular destination and just a few miles off Route 66.

In college, I had the privilege to take an English course entitled, Life and Literature of the Southwest. We studied the Santa Fe Trail and read books centered on Santa Fe. I have enjoyed the stories and art of the Southwest since then, so I was really relating to this place. My personal history was merging with its history.

The monastery and I were both born in the same year, 1948. Trappist monks from Rhode Island originally bought the Valley Ranch and converted it into a monastery. In 1955, they moved to Oregon to establish another monastery and the property was sold to Benedictine monks.

The place looked deserted. It must have been around 5pm in the afternoon and I wondered where everyone was. The double doors with descending doves carved on the outside marked the entrance. "The dove has been a symbol of connections between the unseen and seen world since the days of Noah and the Ark," I thought as I entered the building.

Inside was what looked like a lecture room with several chairs, a podium, and a fireplace in the background. To my right was a hallway that led upward toward the guest services window. I took the right-hand turn and found myself face to face with a nun who was young, dressed in the traditional habit, showing nothing but her face with a black and white background. There was nothing about her face that hinted of beauty. She introduced herself as Sister Mary Francis.

"I'm Will McKinney. Where's Sister Hillary?" I

asked.

"She's in chapel right now," Sister Mary Frances said without much expression on her face. "Are you here for the school of spiritual directors?

"Yeah," I said.

"I will check you in and help you get to your room," she said dryly.

Sister Hillary had been the contact person in applying for the school, so I had expected her. No more mention of that Sister. I was checked in, given my room number with directions and a key.

It was obvious that Sister Mary Frances was not open to conversational chit-chat. She reminded me of a cleaning lady from my hometown who went around town wearing a bandana on her head keeping her hair bound in a do-rag wearing long dresses sweeping to the ground. "Maybe it's the nun garb," I pondered. "Either way, she's plain-looking."

I had already begun sizing her up, as I was prone to do, primarily due to my chosen occupation, I told myself. "Shy? Stuck up? Timid and easily afraid, especially of men?" I wondered. The last thought stuck in my mind.

To save money on the school tuition, I had elected to share a room, so I had a roommate who had already checked in before me. I unlocked the door and pulled my duffel bag on wheels into the room, finding no one there. I could see that my roommate had already moved his stuff in, but there was no indication of which bed he had chosen. I moved my stuff over to the right side of the room and picked the single bed on my right.

I sat on the edge of the bed looking over the packet of information given to me by Sister Mary Francis. Welcome and introductions scheduled for 8 pm. "Surely I can get an evening meal out of this tonight," I told myself. Just in case, I had brought along snacks: peanuts and cheese crackers. "I'm not one to go hungry," I mumbled almost aloud.

As I completed looking over the information packet, someone opened the door to the room and entered smiling. "Oh, hi, I'm Dave, your roommate." Standing in my midst was Brother Dave, as I came to call him, a retired engineer from Washington State, who had just returned from Vespers.

"Have you been here long?" he asked.

"No, only about 30 minutes," I said.

"I was at Vespers," he said. "Are you Catholic?"

"No, Methodist," I said.

"Well, Vespers are the 5pm worship service which is a part of the order of the day, practiced by the Benedictines," he informed me casually.

"Yeah, I was just reading about that in the admission packet," I said. "Are we required to attend?" I asked.

"No, it's optional, I think," he answered.

From that moment, Dave established himself as the resident expert on Catholicism. I encouraged it with my questions.

"Where are you from?" he asked.

"Texas, College Station, Texas, in the central part, about 100 miles north of Houston," I answered.

"You?"

"Seattle area, Washington State," he said. "I thought your accent sounded a bit southern," he added. He was dressed in jeans and a pull over cotton sweater wearing glasses that looked a bit outdated. You know, glass lens get larger and smaller to reflect the current style. Big lens were out. Smaller lens were in. His had the bigger lens. By most people's standards, he was a young, masculine looking guy. Some might even say he was handsome, but I don't measure attractiveness with guys.

"Are you still working?" he asked.

"Yeah, I'm a psychotherapist. You?"

"I retired from Boeing. I worked there for 25 years as an engineer," Dave said.

"What's next?" I asked him, since he seemed to be better oriented than me.

"The evening meal," he said motioning toward the door. "Let's go on over. We can get acquainted as we wait for the bells to ring."

I followed him down the same hallway I had traveled with my luggage after checking in, past the check-in office, through the lecture room, and into a large lounge where several others were standing or sitting drinking coffee and visiting. Apparently, most of the class had already arrived and had been in the chapel when I checked in.

Shortly after we arrived in the lounge, the bells rang from upstairs. I followed Dave and the others up a flight of stairs just outside the lounge and found a large dining area with several round tables and chairs capable of seating about 6 people each. The first person I encountered was a flashy red-head with bright red lipstick wearing jeans and a blue sweater with a white turtleneck underneath.

"Hi, I'm Sherry," she said smiling broadly in such a way that it made her blue eyes look like little slits.

"I'm Will," I replied. In an instant, either a glimpse into an alternate future or a disorienting aftershock of a past life hit me like a subtle earthquake. As it turned out, it was neither of these, but surprisingly close to the later.

"You remind me of someone I used to work with, we shared an office."

"Did you like her?" Sherry asked.

Caught off guard, I may have hesitated too long before answering, "I liked her well enough," I said. "You just reminded me of her, general size and build."

"Oh, so you didn't like her," Sherry said, assuming by my reaction that I was trying hard not to admit any misgivings I harbored for her look-alike.

So, there I was, getting off to a bad start. Sherry's

reaction suggested to me that she was high maintenance, like the former office mate. They both seemed to put a lot of time and energy into physical appearances. Both seemed outspoken and somewhat brazen, in a Bet Midler act and look alike kinda way.

Luckily, other people were pushing up the stairs behind us and we had to get out of the way. I moved down the buffet line where the evening food had been laid out, made my food selections, and found a table over in the corner so I could retreat and regroup.

Everyone was asked to stand while someone prayed over the food. Then people at each table visited while the food was consumed. The food offerings were low budget: eggs, cottage cheese and other dairy products made up the protein selections, fruit and vegetables were abundant, and what appeared to be homemade bread. Deserts were Jell-O products that would have made Marjorie Merriweather Post, the heiress of the General Foods fortunes, proud. It looked like a cross between hospital food and a school cafeteria. No worries, I was hungry, and the tea was good.

After most people were finished eating and people at the table had introduced each other, a monk who introduced himself as Father Andrew, stood up, got our attention, and gave us some basic information about rules of eating there. Tonight, and the first week of school, we would be able to talk and get acquainted. Morning meals after that would be taken in silence. Evening meals would be optional depending on the day of the week and importance in the church calendar.

Following a period of questions and answers, we were invited to adjourn to the lecture room for our first informational meeting. The lecture room looked to be a large living room in the old lodge that had been converted to a classroom. A giant fireplace dominated the wall, which all the chairs were facing. Some chairs were the reclining type, others were rocking chairs, and most were just straight chairs. The general appearance was eclectic, as if some had been donated. A small podium stood in front and to the right of the fireplace.

Father Andrew called the class to order and directed us to introduce ourselves by way of name and point of origin, then to talk a bit about why we had come there. There were 29 people in the class from different states: Hawaii, Maine, California, Washington state, and Alabama, to name a few. Several were from Texas. As a class, we were predominately women and Catholic. Some were still employed, others full-time volunteers, and many already retired. About one-third of the class was non-Catholic. Many had active church connections, priests, nuns, deacons, seminary students, and lay persons. Several counselor-trained people were also in attendance. Some people were in transition between jobs and seeking a new direction. Others were adding to existing skills. Many were encouraged to attend the workshop by friends or church leaders. I had sought this place out on my own, seeking refuge and new learning. As a group, the people seemed flexible, warm, and receptive. I learned that it was the 41st class to be in this workshop and the 25th anniversary of the school.

It took a while for all 29 of us to speak and by the time we had finished, it was time for Compline, evening worship. Most people moved on up the hallway to the chapel, while a few others hung around and visited. I was tired from the early start and elected to return to my room and hit the sack.

*Mother - child*

# 2 settling in

Morning bells rang out to call everyone to rise and prepare for Lauds, the morning church service. Dave was already up and dressed.

"Morning," I called out to let him know I was awake.

"Good morning," Dave said. "I'm on my way to Lauds. Wanna go?"

"No, I like to get a slow start on the day. I think I'll just go the lounge and get a cup of coffee."

"Okay," he said, moving toward the door, "see you at breakfast."

"See you then," I replied, still lying in bed.

With the room, especially the bath, to myself, I rolled out of bed directly to my knees for prayer. This was a part of my routine at the time: prayer first thing, then meditation, inspirational reading, and journal time. After that I attended to personal hygiene matters. Having a beard allowed me to bypass shaving, so a quick shower and dressing for the day put me ready to grab coffee in the lounge. I made a mental note to check out the bath to see how often they were cleaned. It looked like there was black mold in the shower.

This was the first of many trips I would take from my bedroom to the lounge. As I entered the lounge, I encountered a young woman in her early thirties.

"Hi, I'm Will."

"Alisa," she said. "I remember you from last night. You're the counselor."

"Yeah," I said. "And you're the social worker from the Killeen area."

"Yeah," she said. "Is this your first time here?"

"Yes," I said. "You?"

"No, I've been here once before as part of a birthday present. A close friend arranged a trip out here for me just for a weekend retreat. I loved it and chose to return for this school."

"I see you missed chapel," I said, changing the subject. "Are you Catholic?"

"Episcopalian," she said. "You?"

"No, I'm a Methodist."

I could see that she was very perceptive and took her own sweet time in responding. She was in no hurry to get the conversation over with or to make snap judgments. "Humility?" I thought to myself. "Was this a function of her personality or something in her life that shaped this?" I wondered. It was the hesitant responses that triggered these questions inside. I got a feeling she was often late or as they say in East Texas, "a day late and a dollar short."

"What do you think about going to chapel services so often?" I asked her.

"What do you mean?" she said.

"Well, it seems to be pretty frequent, almost excessive, to me. I usually don't feel the need to attend church so frequently."

"Oh, I don't mind," she said. "I like the way they structure the services."

"What do you mean?"

"The men and women take turns reciting the psalms. Sometimes they use piano accompaniment, others are straight a Capella. They have very inclusive prayers and a short sermon. I take communion with them as well, even though I'm not Catholic."

"Well, I'm going to take my time and ease into the whole worship thing. I'm here for a bit of alone time, rest and relaxation," I told her as I moved toward the coffee pot.

"They're pretty willing to let you have your own experiences here," she said.

"Well, I haven't yet had my first cup of coffee, so I'll leave you alone and get a starter cup."

"Yeah, I brought my devotional along to read while I have tea," she said.

And with that we each returned to the silence, quietly sharing the space.

'Comfortable', was the word that came to mind. My impatient self, wanted her to talk and respond faster, but, in all, I found in her a person who I felt comfortable around, even in silence. Patience is the companion of wisdom," I reminded myself.

I am perceptive as well and I'm good at sizing people up quickly. I compare the human personality to that of a football team with up to 100 players or parts included in the overall personality. In my work, I encourage clients to think about the parts of their personality, to name them, and to know how they dominate behavior, emotions, or thoughts and beliefs. Ultimately, I direct them to develop a part that acts like a coach, in charge of each of the other players or parts, and know when to bench them or when to play them. This requires a great deal of self-awareness, along with a strong sense of self-control.

If the sports analogy doesn't work with a client, then I switch to a music analogy using the image of a conductor of an orchestra, made up of as many musicians as a fully funded metropolitan group. I've also used a nautical analogy with a captain in charge of a crew, as well as the body analogy, like St. Paul did in Corinthians when talking about spiritual gifts.

These thoughts were going through my mind as I consumed my first cup of coffee and went over for a refill. Halfway through the second cup, I heard people coming down the hall indicating that Lauds was over. It turns out that the lounge was a hanging out place while people waited for meals to be served. So most people moved into the lounge taking coffee or tea and waiting for breakfast bells to be rung. The silence was over.

Sherry walked over to me and reminded me who she was as she leaned in kissing me on the mouth. Inwardly, I was taken aback as I did my best to appear unshaken outwardly. Why I said nothing, only my future self knew. First, I got off on the wrong foot with her, dodging a potential conflict, and now she was drawing me into a public display of false intimacy. My instincts were raising another red flag that strongly suggested, "Stay away."

She was surrounded by her friends and introduced them to me: Sharon, Arlene, Nerina, and Carolyn. They were all from the Houston area and quickly let me know they were frequent visitors to the monastery, all but Carolyn, that is. They were all Catholic, but Carolyn. She was a Quaker.

It appeared that Sherry was the self-appointed leader of this group of women, but I was making another snap judgment. Carolyn had made a good initial impression at last night's meeting because of her sense of humor and a hint of practicality she demonstrated in her stated reasons for attending the workshop. Sharon and Nerina had caught my eye since they both looked Italian and displayed what I considered beauty. Nerina was the most striking. She took greater pains with her makeup, much like Sherry. Apparently, they had all been briefed by Sherry who I was, what I did, and where I was from (just north of them in Texas).

As the bells rang out calling us to breakfast, I found myself caught up in the group, surrounded by what reminded me as a covey of quails. There was a barrage of questions coming at me from all sides. I answered them one by one until a prayer over the food silenced them momentarily. After the prayer, I deliberately took my time gathering breakfast food on my plate and returned to the table loaded: both with food and loaded to take charge by putting questions back at them. I used the usual getting acquainted questions: "Do you work out of the house?" "What kind of work do you do?" "What does your husband do?" That carried me through the meal, after which I excused myself to make a restroom stop back in my room.

I had not seen Dave very much as he seemed to be giving me lots of space. I interpreted this as him respecting my privacy. My future self already knew that we were developing a pattern of seeing each other seldom during the day and having some pretty good conversations at bedtime as we drifted off to sleep. I liked him.

I had arrived early to the lecture room and picked myself a chair toward the front hoping to avoid the covey from Houston. My notebook was open and ready as other classmates began to filter in. Luckily, Alisa sat on my left and a bearded, older guy with thick glasses and shoulder length hair sat on my right.

"Good morning, Alicia," I said.

"Alisa," she said, correcting me. "It's A Lisa."

"Sorry," I replied.

"Hello, I'm Lorenzo," my seat partner on the right said with a big smile on his face.

"Will," I said. "Meet my new friend, Alisa," I said using this an opportunity to practice saying her name correctly.

Just about that time the abbot entered along with Father Andrew and the room grew quiet.

### *"What do you believe?"*

Our first topic of the day was an introduction to worship at the monastery, led by the abbot himself, Father James. Father Andrew, acting as the retreat director, followed up with the details. The basic message was that all members of the class were welcomed to attend worship, interact with the community and could partake of communion since we were at residence in the monastery for the month. However, each had to believe in the concept of transubstantiation.

The lecture that followed represented what seemed to be a review of the Christian faith from the Old Testament through the gospels. The content focused on Satan, the flesh, and sins of the world, detailing Satan's fall from grace along with Adam and Eve and humankind's pull between good and evil: all have sinned and fallen short of the glory of God.

"The task of spiritual direction is to help directees understand the human condition," Father Andrew emphasized at one point. "It's the task of Jesus to bring us back to God, through the cross and resurrection. Our task is to abide in Jesus by sharing in the cross of Christ and its glory."

The packet of information, I was given by Sister Mary Francis when I checked in, had spiritual direction assignments, as we were expected to receive weekly direction while in the school. Father Sam was assigned to me.

The student in me is a good note-taker. As Father James and Father Andrew talked this morning, I made notes. It helped me pay attention and remember key points. One note I made and boxed in was a topic for spiritual direction later: "guard up – tension up when approached" Translation: My guard goes up along with tension when another person approaches me. I would remember to discuss this with my spiritual director. After all, I had to have something to talk about with him.

During the break after the first lecture, many of us walked outside to enjoy the sun. The weather was cold but sunny. The state of New Mexico was known for its sunny weather, like some 335 sunny days each year. This day was no exception. Lorenzo walked out and sat beside me on the knee length wall just outside by the road running alongside the lecture hall.

"What was your name again?" I asked him.

"Lorenzo, Father Lorenzo."

"So, you're a priest," I stated in an asking manner.

"Yeah, I'm taking a sabbatical to write my memoirs. I am assigned to central America, Guatemala," he said. "I'm currently living in Cleveland, Ohio."

"Well, I'm from Texas, in case you haven't already figured it out."

"I guessed somewhere in the south," he said as he pulled out a small cigar and lit it up with a cheap Bic lighter.

"You smoke?" I asked in disbelief.

"Yeah, a habit I picked up in Latin America. It may not look too priestly, but I don't much worry about that."

It was obvious to me that he didn't worry much about appearances. His graying hair and beard looked untrimmed. His sweater and slacks looked like they came from a thrift store (he later verified that they did). His tennis shoes also looked more like hand-me downs than something the church would issue to their priests. I liked him right away. He had a child-like quality of wonderment and seemed to live in the moment.

The break and cigarillo lasted about the same length of time. As fate would have it, the next lecture, presented by a volunteer lecturer and activities director was about maintaining your health while in the Pecos altitude. Exercise, drink lots of water, avoid excessive use of alcohol (alcohol consumption on site was expressly forbidden) and get plenty of rest. These were the basic instructions. On yeah, if anyone had special health issues, visit the school nurse, Sister Ann, who would monitor your situation.

Two additional organizational items were then addressed: Arranging for times and places to receive spiritual direction and working together in subgroups. The subgroups were already assigned, and we were invited to split up and meet in designated rooms around the building.

My subgroup met in conference room one. We were directed to exit the lecture room and walk outside up the sidewalk around to the east end of the main building. I noticed that one of the covey from Houston, Sharon, was walking hurriedly to catch up with me.

She opened the conversation, "Looks like we are in the same group. You know, I'm a very sensitive person. I pick up a lot of information about people. Sometimes it makes me uncomfortable," she volunteered.

"Oh," I said out loud. Inside, I was thinking, "Too much information…."

"I currently work as a florist. I'm good at arts and crafts. It just seems like people don't warm up to me very well. I'm really not sure what vocation I want to pursue either."

Ambushed. That's what it felt like. I had this happen every now and then, mostly by people who knew what I did for a living. It was like they were deliberately extracting counsel and advice from me, without asking. I generally have a negative reaction to people who take from me without asking, especially when they don't give back.

"I wonder how they will structure the small group meetings," I asked trying to change the subject.

Sharon had occupied my attention all the way over to the conference room. So, as I settled into my chair, I was surprised to learn that the entire covey was assigned to my group. They must have made the assignments based on geography. So, there we were, trailing in: Sharon, Sherry, Carolyn, Nerina, and Arlene. I was the only man in the group.

As we left the main building, we were given handouts with instructions to introduce ourselves and to pick a spokesperson and a group leader. We were to read a pre-selected scripture and discuss its implications in spiritual direction. We went through the process of re-introducing ourselves. Sharon seemed be developing a pattern of asking me baited questions and negating my answers. I felt a growing irritation that usually precedes my anger.

The scripture was from the book of Luke, chapter 24, which focused on the story of the road to Emmaus. In these verses, the story is told of two of Jesus' disciples traveling along the road to Emmaus. Jesus had recently risen from the dead, although not everyone believed that he truly did resurrect. The disciples were discussing this when Jesus started walking alongside them. The message was to meet people, especially your directees, where they were in their faith journey.

From there we trailed off into a discussion about taking communion. Carolyn raised the first question about beliefs and taking communion.

She asked the group, "What does transubstantiation mean, anyway? I'm not sure I believe in this."

Sherry was quick to answer, "It means that you believe that the elements of communion literally become the body and blood of Christ when you take them."

"Huh?" I interjected. "Do you mean literally? Does our DNA change or do we become Christ?"

"That's what I'm talking about," Carolyn said. "I'm not sure I believe that. I just thought we were pausing to remember Christ's sacrifice for our sins."

"Me too," I chimed in.

"Well, it's an individual decision and those beliefs are assumed if you choose to participate in the Eucharist," Sharon added flatly.

"Count me out," I declared.

"I want to consider it further," Carolyn added, as she looked at her watch checking the time. "Class is over," she announced.

As we concluded our meeting, I ducked out ahead of everyone else and headed back to the lounge since it was getting close to lunch. Everyone else headed to the chapel for services before lunch. On my way down the hall, I heard and saw a guy with a thick southern accent dressed in overalls walking ahead of me.

"Who is this country bumpkin?" I thought.

Curious, I followed him down to the lounge. He seemed outgoing, so I introduced myself.

"Hi, there, I'm Will. I couldn't help but notice your southern accent. Where are you from?"

"Alabama, lower Alabama. I'm Sammy."

"What's the difference between lower Alabama and the rest of the state?" I asked.

"Lower Alabama is a geographic distinction we make that includes language and cultural differences."

"Oh, like the difference between East Texas and South Texas people," I said. "I'm from East Texas. You know, we talk a lot alike."

"Yeah, I can tell," Sammy said smiling.

"Well, I get into the lingo more when I'm talking to a fellow kinsman," I informed him.

"You Catholic?" he asked.

"No, I'm a Methodist," I said.

"Me too!" Sammy exclaimed as he raised his voice and smiled even bigger.

Not only was he outgoing, but he seemed a bit dramatic as well. I liked him right away. Although from different states, he seemed very familiar, like family.

"Let me ask you a question," I said. "Do you know what transubstantiation means? Do you believe in it?"

He said, "You know, I was wondering about that myself. Never really heard it talked about in the church circles of Alabama."

"Me neither," I confessed. "Some of the Catholics in my subgroup told me it has to do with believing that the elements of communion, or Eucharist as they call it, actually become the body and blood of Christ. I'm not sure I believe that."

"You mean they believe you or the elements actually become Christ when you take communion?" he asked as if it were an incredible thought. "That we and the elements go through a DNA change?"

"Exactly," I said looking him in the eyes. "I had the same thought"

"Well, I'd like to consider it further," Sammy said in a non-committal manner.

"Maybe we can get together and look it up in their library. I saw a room with a library sign on it as I went over to our subgroup meeting area."

"Okay, maybe tomorrow," Sammy said. "Do you have a private room?" he asked.

"No, I'm sharing a room with Dave. Have you met him yet? He's a Catholic from the Seattle area."

"Oh, yeah. He's the guy who repairs Bibles," Sammy added.

"Really? I haven't had a chance to visit with him very much yet. He spends more time away from the room than there."

"Yeah, he seems pretty well connected here. Maybe it's because of his skill, probably lots of Bibles to repair."

"There's the bell, guess lunch is ready before chapel services are over. We can get a head start and beat the crowd," Sammy said.

"Maybe, but we can't eat before they pray over it," I added.

"No problem for me, we pray over our food at home daily," Sammy countered.

And so, this was the beginning of a close friendship during my stay at the monastery. Sammy was the other Methodist. I learned that he was no country bumpkin, but a radiologist who took early retirement due to an arthritic condition with his hands that prevented him from working. A multifaceted individual, he had become a regular fixture around his hometown church as a volunteer. He found his way to Pecos by way of a recommendation of his friend who was the current bishop for the state of Alabama.

As we made our way up the stairs, the crowd from chapel joined us and we stood around the food and prayed. Rich, a real estate salesman from Wyoming and brother to a resident, Brother Jim, led the prayer. It seemed he had appointed himself as president of our class and spokesperson. I guess he was a natural go-between guy for us. After prayer, we loaded up our plates and found a table. The Saturday food offering was more meager then Friday's. The covey joined Sammy and me.

"I'm Sherry," she said introducing herself to Sammy, without a kiss, I might add.

"Sammy."

To make it easy for him, I announced to the entire table, "Everybody, meet my new friend from Alabama, Sammy."

"Hi, Sammy," they chimed together, like an AA group welcoming a new member.

"He's a Methodist, like me," I added to clarify a question I thought they'd be thinking about.

"What do you do in Alabama?" Sharon asked.

"Oh, I'm retired," he said. "I worked as a radiologist for over 30 years, but my hands got arthritic and I had to quit."

"Does that mean you were a doctor?" Sharon asked directly.

"Yeah, that's the difference between a radiologist and x-ray technician," Sammy said as if he were instructing her.

"My husband is a surgeon," Sherry replied as if to let him know she knew the difference.

In my estimation, Sherry and Sammy were a lot alike. They were both closely aligned to their religion and church, both identified closely with success, and both very ambitious. "What made the difference," I wondered, "that led me to like him and dislike her so quickly?"

My attention drifted in and out of the conversation around the table as a new celebrity caught the covey's interest. By the time I tuned back in, they were talking about going for a hike after lunch. I was up to that, tired from being cooped up in meetings and ready to soak in the afternoon sun. It seems this was an informal plan to allow everyone in the class to get better acquainted. It was suggested we hike the trail up the mountain cliffs behind the monastery and across the river. We gathered shortly after lunch and took off as a group.

Sharon was immediately by my side. Even though she was built in a block shape, she was unusually quick and able to keep in step with me. I stayed in good shape through jogging and cycling, but was not ready for the inclines of the mountains. Either way, she seemed to be able and motivated to keep in step with me. More talk ensued. This time it was more of an exchange, but it felt jerky.

"What do you think about the notion of participating in the Eucharist as a protestant?" she asked.

"I'm pretty sure I won't," I answered.

"Well, you don't have to literally believe in transubstantiation," she countered.

"Literally?" I asked. "When it comes to belief, how else do you believe?"

"You know, symbolically," she said.

"I don't think the abbot meant you have to believe in the symbolism of transubstantiation," I said, feeling my irritation growing.

"Well, how did you like our subgroup experience this morning?" she asked, changing the subject and huffing a bit to keep up.

"Oh, it was okay, I guess. I would have liked to have more people from elsewhere in the group and not all Texans."

"We all have so much in common," she said. "I like the way they formed our group."

It was appearing that Sharon was going to counter everything I said with a different perspective, which did not stimulate a desire to engage with her.

"You come across as guarded and not open enough," she said accusingly.

After some discussion of the matter, offering mostly excuses, I simply asked her, "Bear with me."

So here I was, on only the second day, having a conflicted relationship with two people in the covey. I felt my pace quicken and my breathing become labored as I sought to outpace her. When that didn't work, I simply walked off the path as if to take a picture with my camera or find a place to pee away from the eyes of the group. Either way, it was a ploy to avoid her.

And it worked. After I finally returned to the trail, most of the group had hiked on up. Older members of our group trailed along with younger stragglers who were engaged in deep conversations. I joined an older lady and someone about my age.

"Hi, I'm Will, mind if I walk along with you guys?" I asked.

"Please do. I'm Sister Florence from South Dakota."

"And I'm Zoe from Arizona presently, although I originate from Texas."

"I'm from College Station, Texas," I volunteered.

Oh, yeah," she said with surprise, "I attended Texas A&M University. Are you an Aggie?"

"Yeah, but I was an older student and my identity is not wrapped up in being an Aggie," reciting my standard reply to this question. "What do you do in Arizona?" I asked.

"Teach in a small Christian seminary program," she said. "My husband and I both teach there."

"I live in the Sacred Heart Benedictine monastery in Sioux Falls, South Dakota," Sister Florence offered.

"What do you do there?" I asked risking that it might be a dumb question.

"My training and experience was that of a school administrator," she said. "I'm currently between jobs and living back at the monastery."

"Are you retired?" I risked again. With her white hair and apparent age, it was obvious that she was within retirement range.

"No, I haven't officially decided to retire. I'll wait and see what God has in store for me."

"How about you, what do you do for a living?" Zoe asked.

"I'm a counselor in private practice," I told them. "I'm just getting away for some continuing education and relaxation."

"I do some academic and career counseling in the college where I work," Zoe said. "I thought this school would help me do a better job of advising students."

"I have never been trained in spiritual direction, even though I have received quite a bit," Sister Flo replied. I had already nicknamed her Sister Flo in my mind. I liked them both because they both seemed honest and direct (very comfortable with themselves). No wonder they had already connected and were taking their time hiking up the trail lagging and behind.

"Mind if I take a picture of you?" I asked.

"Not a bit," Sister Flo replied as she stepped close to Zoe and put her arm around her. Both had shed their sweatshirts as the afternoon sun heated them up. Sister Flo leaned on her makeshift walking stick with her left hand and gave a big smile.

"Angelic," I thought. She personified a wholesome, spiritually healthy energy. "A spiritual mother," I thought.

Free from Sharon now, and looking to get acquainted with other classmates, I said "so long" to them and picked up my pace looking to see who was in front of me on the trail.

The next little group was all older and seemed to be lagging for different reasons, mostly health reasons. A little guy sporting white hair and mustache was chugging along slowly behind another man and his wife. She had a portable oxygen tank with her with the plastic mask hooked over her face. A little old lady bent over slightly from age and a bad back slowly led the pack.

"Hello to the trail," I shouted letting them know I was approaching.

"Hello," they chimed back, each as breath permitted.

"I'm Will," I said introducing myself without slowing down much. "Y'all enjoying the outing?"

"James," the little old guy said as I passed him.

"Terry. My wife, Carolyn," the man with his wife offered.

"Phyllis," the little old lady said shyly.

Nobody offered any further conversation, so I kept hiking up the trail moving quite a bit faster than they did. Toward the top, the trail leveled off as I approached a shrine built of rocks with crosses and little trinkets laid around them. The area was surrounded by big boulders that were just small enough for people to climb up on. Most of the group had gathered here and were visiting with each other as they took a breather.

"My husband and I used to ride Harleys," a blonde haired, blue-eyed woman offered, apparently about the sweat jacket I had draped over my shoulders with Harley logos on it.

"Oh, yeah?" I asked. "I have one now and really get a lot of relaxation out of it. I call it my therapy. I'm Will."

"Cindy," she said. "I'm from Iowa."

"Texas," I said.

"What brings you to this class?" I asked.

"I work in a therapist's office who does a lot of work with people who are either borderline or possessed. I'm a support person who sits in the adjoining room and prays for the therapist while the session is going on."

"I'm a counselor in private practice, myself," I told her. "I've never heard of such an arrangement."

"It's pretty different," she said. "A practice that comes from the charismatic Catholic movement."

"I really don't know much about that," I admitted.

"Well, you will get a chance to learn. There's a lot of us here."

Just about then, Dave, gave me a shout. He was standing among the covey group from Texas. I figured he needed to be rescued.

"Will," he shouted again as he motioned me over, getting my undivided attention this time.

"Yeah," I said while walking over his way.

"Sharon said you were like a mountain goat that left her on the trail," he said.

"Not really," I said. "My legs really aren't in shape for mountain trails. I have a question for you guys," I said addressing the group. "Are any of you charismatic Catholics?"

"I am," Dave said. "How about you all?" he asked looking at the covey.

"Yes," all of us except Carolyn," Sherry said speaking again for the group.

"Exactly what does that mean?" I asked. Sammy had joined us showing an interest too.

Dave took charge of the conversation saying, "I joined charismatic Catholic renewal in the '60's and have been a member since. Charismatics can be found in any Christian denomination, but are most often identified with the Pentecostal church. The presence of the Holy Spirit is welcomed much more than in more traditional churches. It's often expressed most in prayer. A charismatic style of prayer is common: praying out loud in church, praying in tongues, raising of hands, etc. Even during songs or sermons, people raise their hands open palm toward the heavens, symbolizing receptiveness to the Holy Spirit. We call these external markers."

"I just thought I knew about charismatics," I said.

"Me too," Sammy added.

Dave went on while he had a chance to complete his lecture, "Internal markers include a radical surrender to the Lordship of Jesus Christ in all parts of life, which includes a strong adherence to the gospels and the teachings of the Catholic Church. We build strong friendships centered on Christ."

"Maybe a bit clannish," I thought to myself.

"Y'all aren't a cult, are you?" Sammy asked, as if reading my mind.

"No," Sherry said, taking charge of the discussion. "We are strongly bonded in our love of the church and Jesus Christ. But even people in the Catholic Church see us as different."

"I find them to be very inclusive," Carolyn said, "as a Quaker."

"Inclusive or into recruiting?" my skeptical Self thought inwardly, but out loud I said, "I've been to Pentecostal churches where they would get all emotional, fall on the floor, and even speak in tongues. Do y'all do that?"

"Yes, and no," Dave said. "We have prayer tongues which are spoken aloud and acquired individually. The actual speaking of tongues is a spiritual gift."

"Yeah, I know," I said with some authority. "I used to teach a spiritual gifts Sunday school class."

Dave didn't address the part about getting emotional and falling down on the floor, so I let it drop. I moved on to take additional pictures of people and wandered up the mountain by myself.

From up there, I could see a view of the monastery. It lay down in a valley, just west of the river. To the north, the valley narrowed into a canyon. To the south, the valley opened to meadows and a man-made lake, which I later learned was called, Monastery Lake. The buildings were generally grouped into three, with a smaller one separate just south of the main building. Another larger factory looking structure was located to the north. Sections of the monastery were connected by hallways that looked like glassed in porches. I had determined that they used solar heating and the closed porches helped contain heat as it was dispersed from one section to another. I stopped to rest, review my pictures and make a few notes in my journal.

The sun was lying toward the west, so I decided to work my way down the mountain by following another trail. Walking alone, I began to feel myself relax into the solitude. A chill was growing in the wind as the effect of the direct sun was lessening. I put my hooded sweatshirt back on and followed the river down to where the trailhead was.

It was growing dark by the time I reached the monastery. Everyone had already gathered for the evening meal and were eating when I arrived. Quickly, I grabbed a plate, loaded it up, and sat at a table where one other person was finishing his meal.

"Mind if I join you?" I asked.

"Don't mind a bit. I'm Father Coleman."

"Please to meet you," I said. "I got separated from the group and was late returning from the hike," I explained.

My excuse didn't seem of any great concern to him. He just continued eating and kept quiet. I turned my attention to my food, while we ate in silence.

Father Coleman sported white hair and a scraggly white beard. He was wearing work clothes and looked more like a laborer than a monk. He seemed comfortable with himself, welcoming but not necessarily entertaining. I was okay with that. When he finished his meal, he simply picked up his plate and silverware and deposited it at the wash window, as we had been instructed to do. No further talk.

After I completed my meal, I followed Father Coleman's pattern and walked back to my room. It had been a long day and I was ready for a shower and some relaxation. I noticed the mold again while showering. When dressed for bed, I opened my journal, made a few more entries, and picked up a pleasure book I brought with me and started reading.

A couple of hours later, Dave walked in the room. "Hey, roommate," he said, announcing himself. "How's it going?"

"Great," I answered. "I'm getting into my novel."

"I was just down in the library, working on a Bible that I'm restoring."

"Yeah, Sammy told me you did that. Is that something you do on the side for money?"

"No, it's more of a ministry and a hobby," he said. "In my world, it seems there's always somebody needing a Bible restored. When it's not the clergy, it's someone with a family Bible, the local library, or an occasional friend or relative."

"I see."

"I'm going to jump in the shower and get ready for bed. It's been a long day."

"Go ahead. I'm just reading while I relax and get ready for sleep."

After his shower, Dave crawled into bed and began talking again. It seemed he was more of a talker than me.

"What's your opinion on Catholic charismatic renewal?" he asked, leaning his head over my way.

I rolled over and leaned back to answer, "I'm trying to postpone judgment. The charismatic exposure I've had already left me feeling a bit skeptical. There is one thing I've been wanting to discuss with you."

"What's that?"

"It's this concept of substantiation?"

"You mean transubstantiation?"

"Yeah, that. Do you believe that the elements of the Eucharist literally change their DNA into the body and blood of Christ?"

"No, the truth is that I really don't believe in that and just don't worry about it when I participate in the Eucharist."

"What?" I asked, almost too loud and with much disbelief. "How can you practice your faith with such a glaring gap in belief?"

"I just don't worry about it," he said, in a tone that I took as a declaration that the subject had been dismissed.

"Okay, I'll have to think about that some more. Good night."

"Good night."

Only my future self knew that the issue of transubstantiation was a core belief separating Roman Catholics from other protestant denominations. Methodists and other protestant denominations believe that communion is an act of remembrance. Anglicans, Episcopalians, Lutherans and possibly others believe Jesus in spiritually present during communion. However, for the moment, I was content just wondering.

*Our lady of the Guadalupe*

# 3 Getting better acquainted

Sunday is a day off at the monastery. It is listed as a DAY OF REST on our schedule. The planner in me had already been considering alternatives, so I chose to skip a general orientation and tour, in lieu of attending a Methodist church in nearby, Santa Fe. It was the first Sunday of the month. The sermon that day was about the time after Epiphany, called ordinary time. At the monastery, the Solemnity of the Epiphany is the title given to this period. Since I am interested in the church calendar, I immediately began to take notes during the sermon. The pastor focused on the letdown after the

Christmas holidays and encouraged people to take the ordinary and transform it into the extraordinary time through the experience of God's grace. Her primary message centered around the notion of sacramental living, explained as living ordinary moments in such a way that the world is better off for our having been here.

I got to participate in communion, as well. No conflicts of belief here. The methods were different than I was accustomed to in my home church. We filed down to the prayer rail, knelt on our knees while another row stood behind and prayed over us with their hands on our shoulders, then we were given the elements one by one. The same procedure was repeated with the behind row becoming the front row until everyone received communion. I liked it, both the novelty and the greater participation of congregants.

Since I declined to participate in the Eucharist, in regular services while at the monastery, this nearby church would serve as my church away from home for the month. I was inspired by the idea of ordinary time and making the most of sacred moments. Since I already had taken my camera along, I decided to record my sacred moments with pictures. From church, I went downtown to the plaza for lunch. While there, I started recording my experiences with the camera.

## *"What is"*

I was becoming aware that alone time and solitude was going to be scarcer than I'd imagined. During these first days, I was sensing that the level of interaction with other people at the retreat was going to be greater than I had fantasized. I could feel the resistance and irritation build every time I thought of it.

"Oh, well," I thought to myself, "wait and see."

The rest of the afternoon was spent in the Plaza area, shopping, hanging out, and searching for a book mentioned by the preacher at the church. I made it back to the monastery in time to relax before Vespers and decided to check out that service before dinner.

It was very enjoyable. I like the way they sing or chant over the Psalms. There was a short sermon presented by Brother John, a monk whom I had not yet met, who had an English accent. Prayers were rather lengthy. They included praying for ancient church saints by name and requests for personal prayers from those present. A surprise ending to prayers assaulted my ears: when most of the crowd went into their prayer tongues. It sounded like a swarm of honeybees working a blooming sage bush in a Texas July. "Drone," I thought to myself, not in the 'lazy and useless' way, but in the 'collective sound,' way. They were 'droning.' Following prayer, everyone was asked to share the peace of Christ with each other. This was done by singling out one another when one said, "May the peace of Christ be with you," while the recipient replied, "And also with you," followed by a hug. They were a hugging group. It reminded me of 12-steppers from the AA program and somewhat like an Emmaus group.

Following supper, a movie, *Shadow Lands*, about C.S. Lewis' life and his struggle with faith is on the schedule. However, Adoration, a time set aside to sit and meditate or contemplate or pray silently in the Chapel will happen first. Choosing to skip that, I walked back to my room to let the meal settle before the movie, lost in thought, "Tomorrow I plan to attend every service except

Eucharist, just to experience it. I still have a problem with the literal idea of taking in Christ's body."

To my surprise, Dave was in the room.

"Hi, Dave," I announced trying to hide a look of surprise when I saw him. "Are you going to Adoration?"

"No," he said. "I'm not much on that part, plus I'm a bit burned out by all the services.

"The day begins with the rising bell at 6am, off to Lauds for first worship of the day. Then breakfast. The Eucharist is celebrated at 7:15am each morning following breakfast. At noon, there is mid-day prayer, followed by lunch. Vespers happen at 5pm followed by Adoration. At 7:30pm the final prayer event happens, Compline. We are free after that for personal study with quiet from 9:30pm to the rising bell," he recited, as if I didn't know.

The truth is that I was still discovering the order of the day. I guess I had just overlooked Adoration in a moment of mind overload.

"I saw you in Vespers," I started, "it was my first service."

"Saw you. How'd you like it?"

"It was very interesting. I enjoyed it. Tell me, what's the noise you guys make at the end of prayers? Is that speaking in tongues?"

"Well, the latter are considered gifts of the spirit, while the former is acquired," he said politely, acting like he hadn't already told me.

"This was consistent with what I've heard, but how are the prayer tongues acquired?" I asked revealing what I really wanted to know.

"It's a part of the mystery. Between you and the holy spirit."

"Can anyone experience this or just people into Charismatic renewal?"

"I guess anyone can experience it," he said, "but I've only heard it practiced in Catholic charismatic renewal groups."

"So, it's unique to your group."

"It's unique to Catholic groups who practice charismatic renewal," he corrected with a hint of authority in his voice while looking at his wrist-watch.

The movie was set to end just in time for Compline, so we continued our exchange while walking over to the library where the movie was being shown. They had popcorn, homemade popcorn in brown paper bags prepared for us. What a treat!

Later that night, Dave wandered in the room long after I had already slipped into bed and turned out the lights. He was in a talking mood and I had a listening ear.

"Are you interested in psychological testing?" he asked as if wanting to know more about my work.

"Not really. I like some of the personality inventories."

"Like the Briggs-Myers?"

"You mean the Myers-Briggs," I corrected with a conclusive tone to my voice.

"Yeah, we took that various times when I worked at Boeing. Management seemed pretty invested in it. I'm an ENTP, if I remember correctly."

"I'm an INTJ. Several Fortune 500 companies have used it. I once contracted for a two-year stint teaching all the police chiefs in Texas about leadership using the test as a basis."

"I'll bet that was challenging!"

"Yeah, the only group more skeptical than engineers are police officers, when it comes to psychology."

"Ever hear of the Enneagram?" Dave asked.

"Oh, yeah, that's my current interest. I've been taking workshops from a nun at a retreat house in Houston for about 4 years now."

"I've also been studying the Enneagram," Dave said.

"What do you think about it?" I asked, now sitting up in bed.

"I like it, especially as it applies to spiritual development. Many of the residents here at the monastery like and use it as well. You know, there's a controversy in the Catholic Church about whether the

Enneagram is Christian based, since its history supposedly came from the Sufi's."

"Yeah, I know. That really doesn't bother me. I guess you have no conflicts over that since you're studying it."

"Not really. It's more accepted among the Charismatic Catholics than mainstream, I think. What type are you?"

"I'm a One, the perfectionist or reformer. You?"

"I'm a Six, the loyal trooper or loyalist. Do you prefer Risso or Palmer?"

"Palmer," I said, "Risso doesn't resonate so well with me. Besides my teacher, Sister Lois prefers Palmer."

"Me too," Dave said. "Wow, we really have a lot to talk about and learn from each other. God must have had a hand in getting us together as roommates."

"Yeah, I feel the same way. Hey, Dave. I wonder if Jesus ever spoke in tongues."

"Good question. Not sure if it's recorded in the scriptures."

" Just a thought," I said. Good night, Dave."

"Night."

Morning sun, shielded by the eastern mountain cliffs, came late to the monastery. I'm up before the bells, showered and ready for Lauds. Dave showers at night, so

I'm showering in the mornings. It all seems to be working well with our schedules. I'm concerned about the black mold in the shower. The cleaning lady was here on Saturday, so I know it's been cleaned recently. Note to myself: 'get bleach next time in town.'

"Morning Dave."

"Morning."

"Have you noticed the mold in the showers?"

"Yeah, I guess. I really didn't pay much attention."

"Well, if you don't mind, I'm going to get some bleach and clean it."

"No problem."

"See you at Lauds, I'm going on over for coffee before they begin."

"See you there."

I'm still thinking about Christ speaking in tongues. In all this charismatic way of worship, it just seems that I'm missing something in my faith if I don't speak in tongues, at least prayer tongues. I realize that I still lack understanding of my faith journey and the workings of the Holy Spirit in it. "Need to check out my assumptions," I thought.

In the lounge, I went straight to the coffee pot, poured a cup and looked around to see who was there. Sammy was sitting over by the couch reading his Bible.

"Mind if I join you?" I asked.

"Sure, come on over," Sammy said with a Southern accent and big grin on his face. "I was just finishing up. How are you this morning?"

"Good," I said. "I had a good night's rest and I'm 'rearing to go and can't go for rearing,' as we say in East Texas. You?"

He laughed. "I'm fine, sleep doesn't always come so easy with me. I've been up since 5 o'clock this morning reading my Bible, doing my daily devotional, and journaling."

"Do you keep a journal?" I asked.

"Yep, especially during this school. I want to keep a record of how God's working in my life during this."

"I also journal, but for different reasons. I have been journaling my dreams for years. Lately, I've been doing stream of consciousness entries in my journal. From time to time, I have insights, ideas, or divine inspiration. I like to record them for later review. By the way, did you ever get a better understanding of transubstantiation?"

"I went down into the monastery library and looked it up in a Catholic dictionary they have there. It didn't really shed any more light on the subject."

"Well, I went to church yesterday in Santa Fe and took communion there. They had a woman pastor."

"How was it?"

"I actually enjoyed the sermon. They did communion differently than I was accustomed, but I liked the difference. What did you do?"

"I hung around and made services here."

"Did you take communion?"

"Yep. I figured me, and God were on good terms with communion. I wasn't going to let the Catholic Church interfere with my participation."

"Great attitude. I'm making all the services today except the Eucharist. I'm gonna warm up my coffee and get some more down before we begin Lauds. See you in there."

"Okay, God bless you," Sammy said. I would learn that this was Sammy's usual way of parting company with most people. This was not in my nature: to be that open to people as a Christian.

As I turned from pouring extra coffee, I saw Alisa. She was dressed for the day and holding an empty cup.

"Let me pour that for you. How are you this morning?"

"I'm alright," she answered as if still trying to wake up.

I poured her coffee and left her alone to drink it while I walked over to the bulletin board with pictures on it. There was a board with the caption: Pecos Class of '03 – Prayer Board. They had put all our pictures, the ones we provided in our applications, on the board. "How novel," I thought. On the opposing wall, there was a similar board showing the various monks, brothers, and oblates associated with the monastery. "A pretty small lot," I thought as I walked out of the lounge toward the chapel.

Lauds, breakfast, another greeting and kiss on the mouth from Sherry, not necessarily in that order. It wasn't a lingering kiss that hinted of a tongue to follow, but more like a handshake or a hug, less than 3 seconds, but lip to lip nevertheless. Like I said before, it was a type of false intimacy. "False," was the operative word that lingered in my thoughts. After a quick trip to the restroom, and retrieving my notebook, I was back positioned for the morning lecture. I had been thinking about Sherry, her motivations and my reaction. After digging deeper in my mind, the best I could come to grips with was that there was something superficial about her, inauthentic. I was consciously seeking more authenticity and found her lacking in that category. "Oh, well," I thought. "Wait that sounds a bit inauthentic itself, like the teen expression: whatever."

Things moved quickly in the lecture of the day. The first talk was given by Sister Ann, who functioned as the school nurse and Father Andrew, the school director. They talked about how to make the best of the experience here and emphasized the use of journaling. Sister Therese spoke on praying from the heart, sometimes called centering prayer. She ended with a meditation exercise that left me zoned out. When that lecture was over, it was time to celebrate the Eucharist, so everybody just migrated over to the chapel.

Taking advantage of some alone time, I quickly journaled the remnants of this morning's dream: *"A flood. Water washed away a lot of sand nearby unearthing an adobe Southwestern church. Doorways and corners trimmed in silver and gold. Placard over door with inscription: I have seen the road to Nineveh. Signed - Patricia L. McKinney."*

Intending to analyze the dream later, I switched to journal another lingering thought from the church service on Sunday: *"How many ways can I make the moments sacramental:*

- *Celebrate the transitions. Life is full of little transitions. I'm sitting in the break room waiting for everybody to come eat. This is a transition – how can I celebrate this time?*
- *By saying grace, being thankful, the Benedictine way. Be more thankful. I'm thankful to have this time alone with my thoughts, with God, by consciously connecting with Christ, by consciously accepting and living in God's grace.*
- *By capturing the moments on camera, recording the moments through various ways, memory and paying attention to detail, journaling, photography, writing notes, cards, etc. Letting others know I'm thinking of them, remembering them, etc. Lost loved ones, connecting to more things, including the unseen world."*

Much of the talk at lunch and during breaks had been dedicated to getting acquainted, learning where people are from and why they came. Often the exchange resulted in sharing resources and/or someone telling their story about what's going in their lives now. At this meal, I met Nancy, a pastoral counselor who is a staff member of a Presbyterian church in Virginia. She, as well as each other person at the table seemed to have something to offer in terms of insights into church dynamics, good resources, and philosophy.

We had the afternoon off, essentially, with an 8pm lecture on the schedule. A few people were scheduled to begin spiritual direction. Mine wasn't until tomorrow, so I had some free time to explore the grounds and out buildings. The warehouse type building housed the print shop portion of the monastery. The newsletter, a monthly publication to keep people informed of events and celebrations at the monastery, was produced in this building. I had been on their mailing list for almost 20 years. Adjoining the print shop was a greenhouse and solar heating section. This was the epicenter of heating for the entire monastery. Adjoining all this was an art museum, housing mostly religious art, that led to a downstairs exercise room. I made a note to myself, "Check out the exercise room tomorrow since it appears we will spend so much time sitting."

The group had already organized at lunch and agreed to meet out front mid-afternoon for a hike up the mountain across the road from the monastery, on the west side. I joined them after my self-directed tour. Dr. Bruce, the featured lecturer for the next couple of days, was our guide. He had come down from Colorado where he taught in a seminary and was obviously acclimated to the altitude and used to hiking. He was a true mountain goat and made me look like the novice I was.

Again, I found Sharon by my side as we hiked up the mountain trail. She was busy offering information and asking questions, "How did you like the lectures this morning?"

"Interesting," I said. "I like the idea of journaling our experiences. However, I expected to have more alone time while I was here."

"I haven't felt the benefits of journaling, but get a lot more out of interacting with people, like they recommended," she said.

Frankly, I found myself tuning her out, knowing that whatever opinion I offered in answer to her questions, she was going to discount it. "Was this how she built her self-esteem," I wondered, "by feeling like she counted more as she discounted others?"

It was a beautiful day and Dr. Bruce expressed what we were all feeling, "What a glorious day and beautiful place that God has made! Let's rejoice and be glad in it!"

On the way back, I zigzagged and deliberately fell behind the group to avoid Sharon and have some time for myself. The trail was well marked, so I felt comfortable about lagging. I had my little pocket journal with me to make notes, so I stopped for a drink of water and time to reflect. I made the following entry:

*Should I feel guilty for avoiding Sharon? I don't do guilt. Anyway, guilt alone is a useless and destructive emotion unless we couple our guilt with repentance and forgiveness:*

- *It distorts your view of self worth*
- *Keeps you from rest/sleep*

*You must acknowledge guilt, then do something constructive with it, then change. Confess, repent, and accept forgiveness. I really don't think I have offended*

*her. It's within my rights to want some privacy. After all,
I told her I wanted some alone time. W.M.*

The group had spread out now as we hiked the last few yards down the trail back to the highway. Dr. Bruce and a few people led the way back to the monastery grounds. Others, grouped up in twos and threes, wound their way behind. I was far behind. From my viewpoint, I could see how subgroups were forming in our class. Sharon, Sherry and the rest of the covey were hiking within hearing distance of Dr. Bruce but seemed to be out of breath in an effort to keep up. Sister Flo and Zoe were just in front of me. It seems they had bonded and preferred to hang back and visit.

Events at the monastery revolved around the order of worship. We were back in time for a short convenience break before Vespers. Then it was time for supper. After that, a short break and it was time for our scheduled 8pm meeting.

Father Andrew led the lecture on how to pray the scriptures. He followed the Ignatian tradition of Lectio Divina, which consists of Lectio (reading a passage), then, Medatio, (meditating on them), then Oratio (praying as so inspired), and finally Complatio (contemplating how to incorporate the inspiration into your faith journey). I had read about it and could acknowledge the reference, but had yet to practice it. "Put this on my 'to do' list," I told myself.

The lecture ended in time for Compline, so I elected to skip out. "I'm backsliding on my commitment to attend all the services," I admitted to myself. Back in the room, I was already in bed by the time Dave returned, "How did you like the lecture on Lectio Divina?"

"I enjoyed it. I've read about it before and plan to practice it as a part of my daily devotions. I have experience meditating and praying already, so it should be easy enough to do."

"Yeah, I have practiced it and usually get useful insights," he said.

"Do you know Latin?" I asked.

"Not really," he said. "Just recognize the primary references used in the old liturgy."

From that our talk trailed off into how the Catholic Church had saved many of the old rituals and contributed to the wealth of knowledge of Christian history. Winding down the conversation, we said our 'good nights' and I drifted off to sleep.

About 4am I awakened from a dream. It was another of those prison dreams that haunted me since I left that job some 17 years ago. "There's a lot of similarities between a prison and a monastery," I told myself as a reason for the dream happening now.

I was unable to go back to sleep, so I quickly dressed in my sweats, grabbed my journal and book, and headed for the lounge. It was like a day room in a prison, a gathering place for residents who didn't want to stay in their bedrooms. This one was open 24/7 and had coffee and tea available. I was surprised to find Alisa seated on the couch reading her book.

"Good morning, Alisa."

"Morning."

"I woke up from a dream and couldn't go back to sleep. Mind if I hang around here?"

"No, don't mind a bit. I couldn't sleep either."

Opening my journal, I turned my attention to making some entries about the dream and impressions about how it relates to my present experiences. After making notes, I decided that I was up for the day and made some fresh coffee. That movement stimulated conversation with Alisa as she paused from reading, "Have you been journaling long?" she asked.

"Yes, I have journaled my dreams for about 7 years and done stream of consciousness journaling off and on for about 5 years now. I was glad to hear Father Andrew recommend it to us, as I'm a big believer of it and recommend it to my clients."

"Me too," she said. "I also write poetry, often as it relates to scriptures. I really liked the lecture on Lectio Divina. Have you practiced it?"

"Not yet, just read about it. You?"

"Yes, I really like it and get inspiration from it for my poetry."

"What a great idea."

Noticing the coffee is ready, I walk over to the coffee bar and pour myself a cup, "Want some tea?"

"No, not yet," she said. "I'm still hoping to go back to sleep before class begins today. I like to sleep late, if I can."

With my coffee in hand, I sit in the chair adjoining the couch and open my book to read. Silence prevails. In about 15 minutes, Alisa got up and went back to her room. I had time alone. I like silence with my coffee. It's a good way to begin the day.

After Lauds and breakfast, I'm in a good mood by the time we gather in the lecture room. The first person I see after I find a seat is Sherry. As she approaches and puts her notebook in the chair beside me, I stand and she plants a kiss square on my lips, saying, "Good morning, Dr. Will!"

"Morning," I said, accepting the kiss, but still caught off guard by her open show of affection. "Show," I think to myself. There is no hug, no holding (longer than a hug), not even an exchange of the peace of Christ, as with ending of services here.

"I'm really excited to hear Dr. Bruce speak. You know, he's a professor at a seminary in Colorado and has a book on spiritual direction that has just come out."

"Didn't know about the book," I answered.

"He'll be here for most of the week and lectures for three days! What a wonderful opportunity to hear an expert speak," she exclaimed with a big animated smile on her face.

"Sounds promising," I said trying to muster up some excitement in my voice.

Just then, Dr. Bruce and Father Andrew walked to the front of the podium and the introduction began. Dr. Bruce had about six inches on Father Andrew. It wasn't that Dr. Bruce was so tall, but that Father Andrew was so short. "Saved by the schedule," I thought to myself.

Today we got more into the meaty stuff, models of spiritual direction, the practice of spiritual direction with all the do's and don'ts, and so forth. Actually, the new book was Dr. Bruce's second book and his lecture roughly followed the material in the recent book. I made a note to myself, "Recommend this book to my friends, Bill and Jimmie."

There was a small bookstore adjoining the lecture room where publications, pamphlets and books were sold, many produced from the print shop. Our class shared an interest in reading new books. As I interacted with others, often, we had read the same books. Sales were good in the store. We were book people. So, the bookstore was crowded during the first break, as everyone seemed to want a copy of Dr. Bruce's book.

This whole business of a community building experience was running against my fantasies of spending a month in a monastery. However, I was facing the realities, slowly. A key word was forming in my mind - "surrender." I had a habit of warring with undesired realities until face to face with, Ultimate Reality. I felt like Jacob wrestling all night with the angel of God, I knew immediately there was no winning the match (when wrestling with God) and surrender was the only option. "How many of us war with God when our plans are contradictory with His plans for us?" I wondered to myself.

After lunch, I hiked up to the hills overlooking the Pecos River. I took a few pictures, journaled, did some rock hunting and took in some solitude. I wanted to be early for my spiritual direction appointment, so I avoided the temptation to nap in the sun. In my haste to get back, I must have left my water bottle behind.

For individual consultation, I was assigned to a priest who was possibly the biggest character in the residential community, having a great sense of humor, wit, and a monk's life style that had the love of God's word woven into the very fabric of his being. He lived and breathed the wisdom of the ages. He was a living example of how the spirit follows the path of least resistance in a person's life. He was a "way shower," leader, a true spiritual director.

My guess was that he was a 'Boss' on the Enneagram, an eight. His Norwegian build and claim to originate from Wisconsin, fit my estimate of him. Farm stock, blocky build, a twinkle in his eye, especially when he looked at you over the top of his glasses. He gave the impression that a sense of humor wasn't the only thing he had cultivated in life.

I had looked forward to the spiritual direction meeting at 4pm, only to be disappointed when Father Sam showed up 30 minutes late.

He apologized, "Sorry, I was busy working on a short homily for tomorrow's service after I finished my nap. The time just got away."

"No problem," I answered. "I used the time to do some journaling."

In a very short time, we covered some very meaty stuff. He had a way of quoting scripture about a variety of topics that let me know he has lived closely with those sacred writings. It seems to be a major emphasis of these Benedictines.

To introduce a personal issue, I read from my previous notes, "My guard goes up along with tension when another person approaches me."

"What's the threat?" Sam asked.

"I don't know," I answered honestly.

"Threat equals stress, which triggers the defensive reactions. Is this life threatening or ego threatening?"

"Not life threatening," I reasoned. "Must be ego threatening."

"Yep," Sam said quietly.

From there, we moved into a discussion of other fears, primarily a fear of putting my family in danger as I move closer to spiritual direction and the concurrent need to stay close to Christ. We discussed prayers of protection that included family and ancestors.

"What else do you want to focus on in our time together?" Sam asked.

"I want to learn how to live more from the soul and less than the personality," I said.

"I must decrease, so He can increase in me," Sam quoted.

"Yes, exactly," I said showing a recognition of the quote.

"How much time do you spend in the word?" Sam asked.

"Not much," I said.

"I challenge you to spend more time in the word, especially the Gospels, and work to make Christ come alive for you in all situations," he said, by using the practice of Lectio Divina."

"I like the sound of it, both in the class presentation and things I had previously read about it," I said.

Father Sam not only liked to quote scriptures, but also often threw out a quote from one of the Christian fathers, St. Augustine being his apparent favorite. My future self would later learn that Augustine blended psychology, philosophy and religion much earlier than people like Carl Jung, but was consistent with this 20th century psychiatrist in blending the rational with the symbolic. Augustine reinforced the idea of living as Christ through the personality and making the experiences last. Father Sam cited his earthly father's words given as he announced he was entering the monastery, "You were my best farm hand." I had a strange feeling of having known this guy for a long time, a mysterious familiarity, like family. "Have I known Father Sam in a past life," the open-minded part of me wondered.

We agreed to meet weekly and set the day and time for our next meeting. At the end of the session, Sam clasped both my hands with his and prayed: "Father God, we ask that you bless our brother, Will, and take the time we had together and transform it into your goodness, in Christ's name, Amen.

That night after supper, I found my way down to the laundry and washed clothes. A book recommended by the lady preacher in Santa Fe entertained me while clothes went through the wash and dry cycles. At 8pm, I planned to attend an informal meeting on 'things spiritual,' so I kept checking my watch."

Turns out the meeting was in the library, just next to the laundry room. The library also housed the only two public computers available where I would go to check and send email during my stay. The topic was about the occult and Satanism. About half the class attended. After an introduction by Father Andrew, he asked members of the class to discuss what past experiences we had with the occult. Several, who had been involved in the Charismatic Catholic renewal movement from the '60's talked about their experiences in the early days. A few were still involved daily working in this area - Cindy's story of praying in the next room while a therapist worked with possessed clients, drew my attention. Then, Pam, also a member of our class told her story of being involved in the occult, satanic abuse, and voodoo.

She said, "I was born into a family who were nomads, moving around from one area to the next. For a while, we lived in the swamps of Louisiana where voodoo was practiced regularly. My people must have been attracted to that culture and wanted to learn more. We worshiped the devil, killed chickens and put hexes on people, dressed up in gypsy garb and practiced magic. It was a way of life and people sought us out to forecast the future, seek healing, or get back at people who had offended them. We made a living doing that. My parents raised me to serve them and programmed me to commit suicide if I ever tried to run away or get out. I had a gift of seeing into the future and knowing how to sense things unseen about others. I was not only schooled to be in their service, but to submit myself in the service of others."

She went on, tears streaming as she gave details of her tortuous years, "On some level, I knew it was wrong. It's no accident that I ended up in an abusive relationship when they married me off. When I escaped that relationship, I knew nothing of a virtuous life. Drugs and prostitution became my way of life. At least I knew how to support myself, on the dark side of life, that is."

She went on, regaining her composure, "In and out of mental hospitals and jail, I became hardened even more. Then I met a priest, Father James, who seemed to understand what the psychiatrists didn't. They had diagnosed me as borderline personality disorder, depressed and suicidal, and suffering from post-traumatic disorder. Medications and talking therapy didn't work. Father James brought up the idea that I might be possessed and when he was appointed Abbot here, I moved here with him."

Father Andrew took the floor again by saying, "Pam has been under our care for three years. After she moved to New Mexico and began working with us, we brought in experts from New York, and-even Africa, to assist us. We continue to do regular exorcisms with her per the Catholic tradition. Since she was programmed, using mind control techniques, she must be under constant suicide watch. This is one of the reasons she is in our class, so we can keep a close watch on her."

Sherry asked a question that everyone was wondering, "How long does it take to free someone from demons?"

Father Andrew patiently answered, "That question has no answer. He who frees is the Lord; who acts with divine freedom, even though he most surely listens to prayers, especially when offered as intercession from the Church."

Alisa surprised me by asking, "How many people would you estimate are possessed by the devil?"

Father Andrew replied, as if quoting a famous exorcist, "Those possessed by the devil are few, but those unhappy souls suffering from adversities, misfortunes, and stubborn illnesses are legion."

I knew next to nothing about exorcism itself. I could relate to the stories of satanic worship and the occult from my prior experiences in working with offenders, both in prison and community probation services. In my private life, I had avoided movies with themes related to the occult believing it was better to protect oneself from exposure to the negative forces of the universe than to be entertained by those themes.

What I didn't know about exorcism was more than what I did know. For example, the gospels cite instances of Christ and His disciples casting out demons, but I didn't know the Catholic Church has a long history of doing the same. I didn't remember that the whole business of Satan and his demons make up a large part of the entire Creation story. I didn't know that NOT to believe in Satan was to leave out a major part of the Christian faith belief system. With a belief in Satan incorporated in the Christian walk, one can re-think the entire meaning of life on earth as a trial of one's faithfulness to God. History, when reviewed considering satanic influence, demonstrates that Satan's power is felt most during times when the sinfulness of the community is most evident. "Currently, consumerism, materialism, and a distorted sense of entitlement is poisoning our culture," I thought to myself. "Where religion regresses, superstition progresses."

If my curiosity had been stimulated enough by the meeting, I would have researched demonic possession to learn that, in its simplest form, possession is about being tempted. Extraordinary possessions, can be categorized into about six distinct types, per Gabriele Amorth in his book entitled, *An Exorcist Tells His Story*. I would have known that one of my prison clients who recited the Lord's Prayer backwards, had voluntarily submitted to Satan, bringing upon himself a possession called diabolical subjugation. I just called it a 'brief psychotic reaction.' I would have known another, who shot and killed his high school principal, was suffering from diabolic obsession. That guy did seem possessed to me. The same would be true for the 'acid freak' probation client who, during nighttime dreams, found himself face to face with Satan who would bargain with him for his soul. His response was to turn to God and become a 'Jesus Freak.' At the time, I thought it was an overreaction, going from one extreme to another. Amorth says the best way to avoid satanic possession is to stay very close to God through the various means of grace.

Further, Amorth says that dreams almost always are influenced by demonic possession. I was reminded of my scariest dream that occurred on August 13, 1985 while working at the prison. It was an indicator that I was under demonic attack at the time. Pam, our classmate, reportedly would be classified as being in the gravest and most dramatic form of affliction, demonic possession, where Satan takes control of the body, as shown in the popular movie, *The Exorcist*. Although my future self would have known all this, I left the meeting remaining mostly skeptical and uninformed. The take-home lesson here: be careful about what you think you know now. As a greater truth becomes revealed to you, then you may find yourself completely reversing your position. It connects to one of my favorite quotes: "To be contradictory is a sign of greatness."

Oddly, a belief in the unseen world contributes to a belief in demons. Augustine had described demons as 'a criminal tampering with the unseen world.' He traced the connection between dreams and demons to Aristotle, Plato's famous student who seriously considered the contention that dreams are scripted by demons.

My future self knows what I did not know then that all the way back to 413, Augustine was talking about God, instead of the gods, and began demonizing the demons, arguing that they are without exception, malign. In his view, they had no redeeming virtues and were the fount of all spiritual and material evil. He suggested they even profess to be messengers between God and man, disguising themselves as angels of the Lord, but pose to lure us to our destruction. "Wow," thought my future self upon learning this, "so long have I considered that it was God sending me messages through my dreams! How tricky this business of evil is."

Popes in medieval times initiated the systematic accusation, torture and execution of countless 'witches' all over Europe. It was mainly girls and women who were persecuted." In Old English, the word 'mare' related to women and girls who had been seduced by demons. Nightmare referred to men who had.

Several of the monks at Pecos were trained Exorcists, Fas. Sam, Andrew, and John, to name the ones I know about. If I had felt more secure, I would have left the safety of what I knew and considered it further. I would have known that the ritual of exorcism follows the usual means to obtain grace: prayer, the sacraments, almsgiving, leading a Christian life, pardoning offenses, and soliciting the aid of our Lord, the saints, and angels. What made one an exorcist in the Catholic Church was to be appointed by the Bishop or greater authority and to learn the ritual, as prescribed by the Church. But I didn't know any of that at the time and had no sense of my future self. That night, I falsely told myself I felt safe, but truly I was spooked by the whole thing. My lack of knowledge fueled the fear and my fear trumped curiosity. It was a catch 22 from the beginning. Goose bumps were the only physiological reaction that I was vaguely aware of.

I did think of a question to ask. "Father Andrew, how do the demons fight against people?"

"The demon fight against you?" he asked in an uncharacteristically challenging manner. "Our own wills become the demons, and it is these which attack us."

No one asked a follow up question. I guess the answer was more apparent than I thought. Even my dysfunctional ex-son-in-law had figured it out some years ago when he said following another failed venture in his life, "I have met my demons and I am them." So, whatever implication that self-will has in the matter of demons was left unexplored at this gathering.

I was reminded of the sermon I had heard on Sunday by the lady preacher. The idea of sacramental living came to mind: cultivating the art of celebrating sacred moments in ordinary life. She encouraged those in attendance to celebrate the transitions of life, such as changing jobs, careers, or spouses, or simply the transitions of going to work, lunch, another meeting, switching projects, and waiting in line at the grocery store. So often we miss the sacred nature of these moments or just get stressed and resort to worry. "Maybe this is another one of those temptations we fall prey to," I thought. "Was this another sacred moment?" I asked myself. If so, it was lost in the fear.

"How can I celebrate the transitions and make the ordinary time sacred in my experiences at the monastery?" I found myself asking again in my journal. Like many questions sincerely asked of the universe, an answer was forthcoming. My mind was already synthesizing what I was learning:

- By saying grace, being thankful, the Benedictine way, be more thankful.
- By capturing the moments through various ways, memory, paying attention to details, journaling, photography, writing notes & cards to others,
- By letting others know you're thinking of them,
- By remembering lost loved ones, etc,
- By connecting to more people in life (including the unseen world).

Back in my room, I crawled into bed, exhausted. "This experience is going to be a lot more complicated than I thought," I admitted in a moment of realization, like Wylie Coyote, the cartoon character when he ran off a cliff in pursuit of the Roadrunner. I brushed off the creeping fear and focused on the coming day. If I had realized the symbolism of the road to Nineveh, I would have known that I was avoiding Nineveh and ended up in the belly of the whale. "Tomorrow is a day off," I thought. There is another planned group hike in the morning and then off to Santé Fe after lunch.

The day had been difficult. I awakened from a sound sleep around 5am with a dream that had an anger theme. As I look back, it had rung a warning bell. We had been prompted to journal dreams while here and to be aware that this place seems to stimulate dreams. Had my future self been accessible to me, then I would not only have been aware, but would've interpreted this to 'beware.' After all, on another level we had been forewarned by Father Andrew and prepped to understand the reasons why when we saw him spending so much time with Pam.

Through the Enneagram, I had learned that people respond to a threat in three characteristic patterns: attempt to avoid it, befriend it, or attack it. I was from the 'attack' response group. Frighten me enough and I go into attack mode. Anger and irritability are early warning signs. Maybe I was unconsciously mobilizing my forces for things yet to come.

The morning sun was obscured by clouds as a low-pressure system moved across the Pecos area. By the time our group hike began, it was snowing. Corn snow, they called it. Instead of snow 'flakes', it looked like small Styrofoam pellets. I concluded that in a country where the sun shines a lot and it seldom rains, it would be logical that the snow would be scant and no obstacle to travel. Sharon was the only woman on this hike. It was a strenuous hike, but she kept up with the group. It seems I just couldn't shake her, and my frustration continued growing. Additionally, I could sense a pattern of my classmates wanting to get 'off campus' with each opportunity for down time. Today was no exception. We discovered the Dairy Queen, just outside of Pecos, a refuge from the refuge.

*Suffering Messiah*

# 4 storming & surrendering

Breakfast passes quickly since we began having this meal in silence each day. I'm learning what it means to participate in community as part of this retreat design. I am expected to live in community with not only the retreat class, but also the resident community, the nuns and monks. However, I did not yet know that the volunteers and lecturers were also considered part of that community. How else could I explain the series of events that happened next?

For two more days Dr. Bruce lectured from his book focusing on Jesus as spiritual director and obstacles to spiritual growth. Father Andrew piggybacked those lectures with an intriguing talk about life initiations and the mystery of Jesus. We processed these lectures in our sharing groups and learned about common models of spiritual growth and development. Our share group stayed on task more this time as we applied the models to where we are and where we have been in our faith journey. I'm more comfortable making deliberate disclosures there and saving my opinions for the larger class gatherings. Sister Miriam finished off the week by taking us through an experiential lecture focused on symbolism and spiritual growth, including using dream content in an artistic manner to discern current issues facing the dreamer.

During break, I made a hurried journal entry: *"Today I was introduced to stages of spiritual development and can see where I am and where I've been. I sense that I am moving toward the next stage, being out into the world serving more, involved with people."*

This last lecture was a primary focus of my quest: using symbols to help people connect to the soul. During lunch, I finally contacted Father Coleman, whom I had briefly met. He is the priest who takes care of the beehives at the monastery. We agreed to go check the hives tomorrow. They have about 20 hives scattered around the area and have had a light harvest this past year due to the drought.

I was also able to talk with Sammy about the meeting about demons. "What did you think about that demon stuff?" I asked him pointedly.

"Spooked me a bit," he confessed. "The next morning during church service, Pam sat behind me. I swear I felt something grabbing me on the back from behind."

"Well, the whole thing unsettles me a bit," I concluded, hearing the warning bells ringing again in my subconscious mind. "Let me know if anything else strange happens."

"Okay, I will. God bless you," he said as we parted.

A special service was offered this afternoon, just for our class. At least this is what I first thought. It turned out to be a special worship service that required us to conduct the service. Karen, whom I nicknamed, High Pockets, because of her high waist, led the procession carrying a cross as we marched outside the building and upstairs to the chapel. Alisa played the piano. Terry, a deacon in the Catholic Church, read the scriptures. Father Lorenzo led the service by offering the Eucharist and giving the homily. This time, I did participate.

The service lasted almost 2 hours and ended with a classmate, Jim, having a medical crisis. Later, it was determined that he had a mild heart attack. The average age of the class is about 55 or so, with only 2 women younger than 40. The ratio of men to women is about 1:4. Jim spent 2 nights in the hospital and was released back to join the class.

Did I say I participated? That means I took communion. That act symbolized my willingness to buy into the symbolism of transubstantiation. It would take me several years to realize the self-conducted worship ritual was a way for the class to experience coming together as a community, a church of Christians from different denominations. Looking back on it, I'm glad I did participate by taking communion.

Additionally, I joined our small group for a short hike just after breakfast. Yes, in addition to participating with the larger community, I'm also making a conscious effort to join in with the group. I was probably motivated a desire to prove Sharon wrong after her accusation of my holding back. Paradoxically, it seems as I surrender, we are bonding somewhat and avoiding contentious discussions. Further, as I surrender, I am experiencing more sacred moments by being in the present, rather than past or future. There is peace in this, this surrendering. It's what M. Scott Peck called 'emptying oneself.'

Father Paul, whom I had only visited with briefly, interpreted the results of the Myers-Briggs Type Indicator (MBTI) which we had taken the first week of residence. No surprises there as my profile has been the same over several occasions. I was not impressed with Father Paul's presentation: he appeared very nervous and was superficial in his explanation. I had shared with him my prior experience and expertise. "Do I intimidate him?" I wondered inwardly.

Sunday, a designated day of rest, offers another opportunity to seek 'refuge from the refuge.' I have dubbed the Dairy Queen with this nickname, a special designation that incorporates the 'Texas rest stop' advertising campaign. No classes today, so I passed up the movie and popcorn that was offered in the library and went to church in Santé Fe with my new friend, Sammy. I found myself really enjoying the pleasure of his company. With him, I felt safe even though we were both spooked a bit by the talk of demons. After church, we spent the rest of the day together sightseeing in Santé Fe and joined Sharon and Sherry, from our class, for dinner. It was not planned.

Sammy, "What do you want to do?"

"I'd like to hang around the plaza, shop for jewelry for my wife, and find a cigar shop," I offered.

"What kind of cigar do you like?" he asked.

"I'm not zeroed in so much on a particular brand," I replied. I do like a Cuban cigar when I can get one."

"We once took a cruise and stopped near an island close to Cuba. There was a Cuban guy there rolling handmade cigars. As I remember, it was a Cohiba," he said.

"Alright then, that settles it," I offered. "Let's go around the corner and see if I can find the cigar store I saw last weekend. I'm buying a couple of Cohibas."

After that, we stopped at a jewelry store next door and I found a nice locket made of turquoise for my wife. It would please me to see it on her. That's how I chose jewelry for her and it seemed to work consistently because she regularly got compliments when she wore something new I had purchased for her.

Sammy is a very intelligent Forrest Gump, a jewel of a guy and a great pleasure to spend time with. We talked about Viet Nam, his experiences as a combat physician. We talked about his son, Samuel, the third. We shared feelings and thoughts. I loved his Southern expressions. We shared food.

"One thing I would like to do while we are in town, is to have a steak," Sammy said, rubbing his stomach.

"Okay with me," I said, with the meager food offerings of the monastery in mind.

So, as we were asking around for directions to a restaurant that served good steaks, we encountered Sherry and Sharon at the Indian Market. Rows of Native Americans were lined up with their products offered for sale. Many things were laid out on colorful blankets. The impression was that everything was handmade by the salesperson. The four of us strung along the full length of the sidewalk on that side of the plaza looking at the crafts. By the time we all came together at the end, Sammy had directions to a restaurant just the other side of the block away from the plaza. He, being the ideal masculine figure, he was politely asked Sherry and Sharon if they wanted to join us. Of course, they agreed. So here I was, doing my best to avoid these two, and finding myself about to have dinner with them!

"If I'd only told Sammy of my frustration with them," I thought. "Oh, well," and with the very next thought, "here's another opportunity to practice surrender."

My steak was memorable. It was cooked to perfection, tender and juicy, "Finger lickin' good," as we would say in East Texas.

The accompaniments complimented the entrée, very nicely. Conversation was kept superficial and often referenced 'things religious.' Sammy was good at this and Sherry was too. Sharon tended to make it more about herself and drew the others into offering suggestions to her that she could reject or oppose. I kept quiet, enjoying the meal. Afterwards, we walked around the Plaza while I enjoyed one of my cigars. This was not an intentional way to create space, but it yielded the same outcome. By the time we found a Hagen-Daz shop and enjoyed an ice cream dessert, Sharon and Sherry realized that they had lost touch with the rest of their group.

"You guys can ride back with us," Sammy offered politely.

"What?" I asked myself, wondering if he was out of line. After all, he was riding with me.

"Yeah, I have room in the truck, if you guys need a ride back," I added to make the invitation official.

"Yes, we'd appreciate that," Sherry said in her own polite manner. Sharon nodded and smiled.

By the time we walked to the place where I had parked the truck, Sherry and paired off with Sammy, talking as they walked. I was left with Sharon. When the doors to the truck were unlocked, Sherry jumped in the back with Sammy and Sharon got up front with me. The drive back to the Monastery was full of chatter and we pulled into a dark parking lot near our rooms. If anyone observed us, they might have concluded it was the four of us returning from a date. Was that a date? I think not!

All I know is that by the time we got back to the monastery, I had made peace with Sharon, I think. It's like jerking a rope held by two people. It's difficult to have a jerking contest when one of the two releases grip on the rope. I let go of my grip.

It was late when I got to my room. I went in and slipped into my bed without waking Dave. I really didn't want to talk with him that night – not without thinking it through anyway.

## *More Storms*

Monday brought more classes. We discussed the healing of childhood wounds and inner child work. We had two meditations that were very relaxing. I enjoyed this because I had not slept very well that night. I had kept waking up. Although my experience was relaxing and enjoyable, the critic in me was not impressed with the content and approach to inner child work.

After lunch, I skipped out for the afternoon for a lengthy hike with Karen the Deer, had invited me to accompany her. She was a retreat volunteer, who I began to think of as 'The Deer' because of her way of hiding in the shadows, hoping to be noticed. Her stated reason for the invitation was to show me a good place along the river to search for rocks, I wondered if it was for solutions to her personal problems. It quickly turned into a counseling session. I am coming to grips with this as part of God's purpose for me here. "Is God answering my prayers through these people," I wondered.

My theme for the moment has been 'surrender' and I am learning to go with the flow. As I mentioned earlier, I had done active reading on the Enneagram and spirituality. Since Dave told me Karen, the Deer, was also studying the Enneagram, I halfway expected her to bring it up during our hike, but she didn't. So, I'm just relating and being curious.

"There's a bend in the river just upstream that has lots of big rocks and exposed tree roots," Karen offered, taking the position of a guide. She was dressed in jeans and a tight-fitting sweater with a rather large cross hanging from a sturdy chain.

"Okay, I like rocks," I answered and followed her lead.

"Many of these rocks are granite," Karen offered as we approached the bend in the river. "Let's make an altar," she suggested and began picking up suitable rocks without waiting for me to reply.

"Okay, here's a big one that will form a table top. We can use a couple of smaller flat rocks to balance it on," I added, picking up the big rock, barely managing to move it around because of its size.

Once built, I picked flowers to put on the altar's top and we prayed together dedicating the altar to God. The property was dotted with small altars, crosses, and grottos, each a symbolic offering of gratitude and reverence to God. I spotted a tree along the riverbank whose exposed roots were twisted around a small boulder and took a snapshot of it. "I wish I could have this with my husband," Karen said sadly.

" You don't share your faith with your husband?" I asked, with a look of surprise on my face.

"No, he's very skeptical and not even sure if he believes in God. At best, he's agnostic, if not an atheist," she said with tears welling up in her eyes.

"Too deep to soon," I told myself. She was providing too much information too quickly. We had only recently become acquainted and there was no formal counseling relationship. A master at knowing when to go deeper into a person's troubles, I took it back toward superficiality by bringing her to the present, "Let's just leave this at the altar today and enjoy the trip back."

"Okay," she replied. If she noticed that I had taken over as the guide, she showed no indication of it.

I led the conversation back to nature and the beauty of the place as we returned to the buildings. Karen, the Deer took a few pictures and I took one of her standing in the shadows, as if hoping to be noticed. I was impressed with her artistic eye and ability to frame the pictures she took. So, a few compliments and a lot of talk about photography dominated the talk all the way back to the building where we parted.

In reflecting on the day, I made the following journal entry: *The Enneagram book I just finished encourages the reader to let go and let the creation that God made in us to manifest itself. I learned that like Jacob, I have been wrestling (warring) with God. I laughed at myself when I realized that I can't win, wrestling with God. Therefore, my only option is to 'surrender.' Instead of 'warring' with others, I have been mindful that 'surrendering' is an option. Instead of avoiding ministering to people with problems, I have been consciously accepting it. Like flashcards presented to me repeatedly, I am gradually finding the correct response. Consequently, I have a growing sense that my mission is to assist wounded people here, to minister to them. Actually, I am feeling renewed for the first time today and am opening my heart and mind to the idea of nurturing others.*

Tonight, we had a first demonstration of a 3-day dance and movement ministry. This was very new to me. Initially, like a clam, I was closed to the idea, feeling incompetent as a dancer. However, it was surprisingly easy and enjoyable. We also did an exercise of giving childhood wounds up to Christ by writing a letter to God. There were many tears and some people were quite surprised about breaking down emotionally. The leaders were a man and wife team who had international experience.

Each night Dave, whom I had come to call, 'Roomie,' processed our thoughts for the day's lecture experiences and shared knowledge about the Enneagram. It had become our weekday rhythm established early on. We mostly were sizing up the types we thought classmates fit in and gave clues that made us think so. It was a good way to drift off to sleep and grow closer together.

By now, I'm making all the gatherings of the church services, except the Eucharist. I love citing the Psalms with the community. The homilies are hit and miss in quality. I'm feeling a sense of home in the coming and going. This is the one place where everybody there comes together, and I feel like I belong there. However, I still have some lingering hesitation about participating the Eucharist if I don't really believe in transubstantiation.

Only my future self knew how much surrender God required of me. I was reluctantly emptying myself of preconceived notions of volunteers' role in the community while tests of my rules for teachers were lying in wait. Some people still believe that their agenda was more important and reputation more significant than the Divine.

The next morning, we have a lecture by Father Wolf, who is both a parish priest and licensed counselor. He is speaking on depth psychology, confidentiality and duty to warn, ethical issues in spiritual direction. Sherry meets me in the lecture room with her usual kiss and cheery greeting. I tolerate it still.

As Father Wolf lectures, it didn't take long for him to get into trouble with the fundamentalists in the class over the subject of homosexuality. One class member walked out after he singled her out in front of the class. She and others challenged him on the scriptural basis for his support. I labeled them, 'scriptural confronters.' I found myself in the unfamiliar position of class mediator, to prevent an unhealthy class polarization. After we got past that, Father Wolf gets into the issue of duty to warn, in the case that a directee shares suicidal thoughts. He advises us that we should never share that information with anyone else. In my opinion this is wrong, just flat wrong. So, I challenge him right in front of the class. I was taught differently and considered myself current on the cases that made it clear that we, counselors, had a duty to warn. I thought he had the obligations of a priest confused with his counselor's duties and was giving out misinformation. Father Wolf obviously was not used to having his authority challenged. So we had two episodes of open conflict in front of the entire class.

"Father Wolf, I disagree with your position on keeping suicidal communications confidential," I said, standing to make myself visible in the class and to him as I also raised my voice. "This advice runs counter to everything I've read and been taught."

Apparently, surprised and caught off guard by the confrontations, Father Wolf got defensive, "By what authority do you base your comments on?"

Armed with experience and research, and fueled by righteous indignation, I let him have it full blast, "I'm licensed as a professional counselor and marriage/family therapist and have taught classes on suicide to hotline volunteers and other counselors. I also worked in Texas prisons at a first offender unit where suicide attempts happened on a regular basis. I have also been trained at the Menninger Clinic in Kansas on the topic."

"What's your recent training and experience in suicide prevention?" I asked, squaring off toward the priest.

Having established my own authority to speak, Father Wolf, now red-faced with embarrassment or anger, wisely chose to move on, "Well as a priest, I don't have the option to break confidentiality and the practice of spiritual direction has yet to address this issue formally. Further, when they are under my care, I don't expect them to act on suicidal thoughts."

Believe it or not, I let his last comment slide. Only once in my career had I heard such an arrogant comment by a therapist. I considered that one to be a narcissist!

The discussion tapered off into pros and cons of Codes of Ethics and basic Christian duties. I knew there were other therapists and psychology trained helpers in the class. Why they chose to remain silent was a mystery to me. I felt no support from them or the rest of the class. I did feel alone, a familiar feeling of standing alone that haunted me far too frequently. "Both alone and misunderstood," that how it feels, as I critiqued the situation to myself.

However, Bill, the husband of the dance instructor couple, sought me out during the break and said, "You were right taking that stand. It was obvious to me that you would not sit and remain silent when critical misinformation was being given to your class." Anger and courage are the daughters of hope," he said. Anger at the way things are, and courage to see that they do not remain the way they are. It was a hopeful act."

"Exactly!" I replied with the passion that comes when someone voices what you only know instinctively and emotionally. "This guy gets me," I thought to myself. We became instant friends.

"I need to blow off a bit of steam. Bill, would you like to go off campus and walk down to Pecos? I'll spring for lunch."

Bill seemed equally ready for a break and quickly replied, "Yes, anyone else interested?"

"I'd like to go with you fellows," Father Lo chimed in. "I'm out of cigars."

"Okay, let's go. Maybe we can find something different to eat in town. I'm buying," I offered, feeling very generous now.

So off we went, debriefing the conflicted issue of breaking confidentiality and finding areas of mutual thought in between the polar extremes. The walk to Pecos was downhill and the mile or so there went quickly. We found a little diner that offered the traditional food of northern New Mexico cooked by the wife of the mom and pop establishment. Father Lorenzo surprised me by having a beer with lunch. So I followed his lead. We both purchased cigars at the little Stop and Go station on the way back.

A full stomach, a beer and the upward slope made for a more difficult hike. We were more silent, but content.

The electricity in the air seemed to subside after lunch. It also helped for the class to spend about two hours in another expressive dance and movement class. Feeling closer to Bill, I felt myself letting go and giving myself to the dance with greater abandon.

During break, I stole some time to myself and made the following journal entry while it was still on my mind from this morning: *"Consciousness clings to the ego until it (the body) dies, either the physical body dies or is at rest (like in sleep), or when the consciousness is altered. Altered consciousness is sometimes the best we can do in this life, it frees us somewhat from the ego. A God-consciousness connects us with the collective/connective unconsciousness."* These insights were fleeting and mostly blinded by my present egoism. Only my future self could see how my self-appointed righteous stands that left me feeling alone, unsupported and cast out of community, was of my own doing. It was a sin unique to perfectionists, who were overconfident in their sense of rightness. It was built into my false self and needed to be emptied out, but I couldn't see it at the time.

This evening an optional healing and anointment service is offered. I decided to attend. We began with a brief explanation of what was about to happen and, then, we simply lined up waiting to see the priests. There were two priests, therefore, two lines. I got in line to see Father Sam, my spiritual director, toward the end of the line. I observed people coming to the priest, who spoke to the class participant mouth to ear, anointed them, and prayed over them. Behind were two other class members waiting to support the recipient of the anointing who, on occasion, fell backwards, as if slain by the Holy Spirit. When it was my turn to go, Father Sam anointed me after I confessed my sins to him and pushed the butt of his palm against my forehead until I fell backwards into the hands of the two supporting classmates, who lowered me to the floor. I took this as symbolic of trust and surrender, but felt no 'striking' down by the Spirit or instant healing. However, since then I have felt something like a healing. Through the process of journaling my future self has assembled the fragmented insights into a mosaic showing me that unique nature of my sins, playing God through the process of self-righteousness.

Throughout my time at the monastery, I've gathered that Father Andrew and Father Sam started working with Pam, initially. As Father Andrew explained to us in that alarming evening meeting, they brought in specialists in exorcism from Africa and New York City. Many of the residents of the monastic community believed that this brought the entire monastery under spiritual attack, requiring that the place and the people be engaged in spiritual warfare. For the community, itself split on this decision, this has meant quite an upheaval, with many of the members leaving and relocating elsewhere over the past two years. This is why so few residents remain with the community now. One priest reportedly married a nun and left altogether. In response to the energy stirring inside of me at the thought of a spiritual attack, all I can say in response is this, "Please pray for the safety of me, my family, and the rest of the class."

Some of this information has been gleaned from nighttime discussions with my Roomie, Dave. Tonight, he is unusually quiet. No problem with me, I like quiet. "I wonder if he was a bit turned off by my showing my confrontational nature." I pondered on this as I drifted off to sleep.

The days are moving faster and tend to merge as more lectures and information is presented. My resolve to practice Lectio Divina has weakened with the process of surrendering to 'what is.' Today, Sister Hillary, who has a Ph.D., lectured on St. Theresa of Avila, focusing mainly on her metaphor of the Castle as symbolic of the inner workings of the soul. It is one of the better lectures. Another good session of spiritual direction with Father Sam helped resolve some childhood fears centered on Pentecostal church services. The charismatic theatrics here had stirred up those old fears that I thought had been put to rest.

In connection with this, we discussed fears of 'things demonic' in a spiritual direction session. Father Sam refrained from easing my fears, and said, as if quoting some other authority, "It's not the marketplace where demons hang out, because only a few are needed at the corner of each square, but the monasteries and religious places, wherever God is working, is where the demons hang out in numbers attacking the innocent souls dedicated to doing His work."

"Wow," I replied. So, we may be in much more danger here than back home living our daily routines.

A day off on Wednesday gave the class a chance to escape off-campus again. Some toured historical sites in the area while others hit the trails for hiking and outdoor exercise. Santa Fe and New Mexican food beckoned me back to the city. I had plans to get back by 2pm to do some personal devotional study, but they were abandoned after an unscheduled stop at the Harley store and the opportunity to ride a V-Rod, a new, super-charged motorcycle. Dave and Sammy accompanied me, waiting while I took the Harley for a spin. Later, we ventured over to Canyon Road for an outside lunch and a mosey around the art galleries. Upon arriving back at the monastery, I realized that I had left my camera and bag at the restaurant. Sammy rode back with me to retrieve it from the manager who held it for us. By the time we returned, the entire day was gone. I had stood up Father Coleman.

Thursday, Friday, and now Saturday greets us. After some regular hiking and walking the running trail, I got my first good run in today. I logged in about 3 miles and held up well, considering the elevation. I am acclimating here. The spiritual follows the path of least resistance, like surrender. I think it's the other way around with the physical, like being willful.

Day's end was greeted by a beautiful full moon in clear skies and found the class gathered with a campfire down by the riverside. "Was it Alisa's idea?" I wonder. It slips my mind. Anyway, Father Lorenzo emerged as the impromptu leader and entertainer of the group. He was dressed in cold weather clothes, probably from a thrift store complete with leather coat that resembled a high school letter jacket, gloves, toboggan, and khaki pants. His long grey beard and thick black-rimmed glasses made him look authentic with the campfire burning beside him. Initially, Father Lo (as I nicknamed him) sat on a log and whittled, beginning one of his many stories, "You know I served the poor in Guatemala, away from the cities. We traveled to the small villages that were so remote and poor that they could not afford a regular priest. When we arrived in the area, word spread quickly and by the time we approached town, people lined up alongside the road cheering and welcoming us there."

"We were revered and subject to little judgment over how precise we were with the liturgy. They we just happy to have a priest there to bless us, christen the babies, and provide the Eucharist," he continued.

"It was here that I learned how rich poor people are in community. They were good in entertaining themselves even though they had few material possessions. Just like whittling with this knife," he added, "it was a luxury just having one to whittle with."

"Of course, telling a delightful story got you lots of attention in the community because you could entertain and impart values of the community. A good storyteller would often compete with a priest, in terms of influence. A priest who spins a good story was highly loved by the people. I sought to become that priest," he concluded.

Little did the class realize that he was using the same charms to win us over. He proceeded to lead us in song, songs that we all knew, and then lead us into new ones that had a South American origin. We laughed, cried, and bonded with his jokes, stories and songs. By the end of the night, he had us in the palm of his hands without any conscious effort. We knew how poor we were by his example. Father Lo was just that kind of guy, an example of a modern-day Christ figure.

While Father Lo had emerged as the unconscious spiritual leader of our class, Rich had consciously appointed himself as the organizational class leader. For some reason, he had sought me out for bonding. Rich asked, as the campfire crowd was dispersing, "Will, mind if I accompany you to church tomorrow?"

"No, not at all," I replied. "Meet me on the parking lot about 8 in the morning. The service starts at 8:30am."

"I'll be there," he said.

I walked back to my room following behind the pack sorting out my feelings about Rich's interjection into my life. Like Sherry, he had caught me completely off guard. It's doubtful I would have offered an invitation myself, thinking he was uninterested in protestant religions and he was so, well, 'Catholic.' It was an unsettling end to a very enjoyable evening.

Sunday began with plans to attend the local Methodist church again, this time with Rich, the Catholic guy. However, God often changes our plans. In this case, Susan, another class member was accidentally poked in the eye with a burning stick at the campfire. Initially, she thought she was okay. During the wee hours of the morning, she came to the coffee room complaining of pain in her eye and hadn't slept all night.

Susan, crying with her right eye closed shut and tears streaming down her face, exploded with emotion, "I thought it was just a minor poke, but it just kept hurting and became so intense through the night, that I couldn't sleep. This morning, I decided that I need to have somebody look at it. It's just more than I can tolerate!"

Alisa and I were up and having early coffee when Susan came in full of distress. We both had noticed that she was already quite emotional and dealing with the aftermath of a divorce, in which her physician husband had left her for a much younger nurse, a woman who worked in his own office. Susan had a few emotional breakdowns during the workshop experiences and had been surrounded by the covey, who had laid hands on her and prayed over her. I had chosen to respond by being a quiet presence who silently provided comfort, a prayerful attitude, and sent positive energy her way. Accidently, I had stumbled upon the ministry of presence.

So, Alisa and I summoned Sister Ann, the school's nurse, for assistance. She came quickly and determined that Susan needed to be seen by a physician at the local emergency room in Santa Fe. Alisa and I, both trained psychologically and experienced counselors, agreed to accompany Susan for emotional support. It was obvious that the physical pain aggravated the emotional pain Susan was already experiencing. A male and female balanced out any question of impropriety that might have surfaced had I gone by myself. It turned out to be a helpful decision because at that time Suzie was so emotionally fragile.  The covey led the entire class by acting out charismatically in such a way, through the laying on of hands and praying, that it reminded me of the birdlike creatures in the Harry Potter stories who sucked the life out of people, "what were they", I wondered, "oh, yeah, dementors." If only my Future self had cautioned me about being so judgmental and foretold my future actions in laying on of hands and practicing Reiki….

Anyway, we finally got her examined and she was released with instructions to keep the eye medicated to avoid infection and to take pain medications, as prescribed. We filled the prescription at the clinic and were on our way back to the monastery in time for lunch.

We found the place quiet since everyone seemed to have gone somewhere else. At 2:30pm, I was finally able to meet with Father Coleman, the resident beekeeper, and do a winter check with him to see how the bees were managing. One hive was dead, and we used the remaining honey to feed the other hives.

"Where are you from originally?" I asked, while we worked.

"The Midwest," Father Coleman replied, without stopping or looking at me. He kept working without offering any more information, so I inquired some more.

"What did your parents do to make a living there?" I asked, continuing to work without stopping to look directly at him.

"We were a farming family. There were 12 of us kids," he added.

"Wow," I replied, stopping to look at him briefly, "I thought I came from a large family. There were 7 of us."

"Well, it was customary to have a lot of kids growing up at that time and place as Catholics who were farmers," he offered, seeming to open up a bit more.

"Yeah, same for us, even as Methodists. I guess it was the farming thing. I was one of 5 boys, which almost insured that there were plenty of laborers around to do the farm work. That is, until my mother died, and we had to move to town."

"We were poor and there were few options in our family at that time. I have always felt a desire to serve God, so it just seemed natural for me to become a priest," Father Coleman said, still keeping his focus on the work at hand.

"Me too, I have a collection of poor boy jokes," I offered, testing his sense of humor.

No response from Father Coleman, so I dropped the attempt at humor. The work was enjoyable. We both knew what we were doing, and he instructed me in the perils of beekeeping in bear country. Most hives had to be fenced off to keep bears out. Even then, some would break through the barriers. It had been almost 18 years since I kept bees, but had accumulated up to 20 hives over the 14 years I was involved. That activity had ceased because of another event in my life, a divorce.

One of my early beekeeping books was entitled, "The Gentle Craft." Father Coleman personified that gentle man working his craft. He has spent much of his life in service to God.

"I was fortunate to be able to serve in Mexico for much of my priesthood under the support of the monastery," he said, breaking the silence of the labor. "I returned about 10 years ago because they needed me here."

"It looks like the number of residents is dwindling," I added, quickly.

Father Coleman comes across as somewhat simple and slow, but it turns out that is deceptive because when he does talk, he often reflects some profound thoughts. He chose to remain silent to my leading comment and, instead, after a long pause, said, "Remind me some time to talk with you about my ideas on social justice."

"Okay," I replied, making a note to myself to remember to follow up on this.

My primary goal upon coming here has been to learn about how to live beyond my personality and body and live more from the soul. Today, I feel I am on track. While in Santa Fe, I found a book that I feel represents the next step, entitled, *The Power of Now,* by Eckhart Tolle. It addresses the practical methods of living more from being, instead of doing with the mind and body in charge. I bought the CD series, so I could listen, stop to take notes, and access it on hikes as well as while driving. Many people were reading or had read it in our class and were giving it high praises.

It was an eventful day. Dave and I processed the events as we trailed off to sleep. For a change, I had more news than Dave, who listened intently.

*Resurrected Messiah*

# 5 Saturation

I was up at 6am today and able to make it to 6:30 Lauds as the New Mexican winter sun was lighting up the eastern horizon just below the cliffs. I have a break before breakfast. I am having so many new and different experiences (of religion) everywhere I turn. I have been exposed to the Catholic and charismatic rituals, the Catholic doctrine, all of which are new ways of thinking and expressing faith for me. Between the books, I am reading and perusing, and the social interactions, the impact of formal classes is waning a bit. Simply spending time with people like Father Coleman or Father Lo, who live from the soul and are concerned with Being (as opposed to doing), points me in the direction of modeling them, which has been a goal all along. So, regardless of the quality of any single lecture, or the collective teachings, I am feeling fulfilled these days. There is an abundance of sincerity and love here. Maybe that's why I keep telling myself that I feel safe here (a possibly more interesting question would have been, "why do I need to keep reminding myself I feel safe?"). My future-self possessed the only answer at that time: there is a primitive, instinctual self that knows when in danger and acts or responds beyond thought.

Class today is on spiritual gifts and charismatic prayer. I'm primed for this, since I have previously taught classes at our church on spiritual gifts. Sherry greets me as she walks into the room and gives me another kiss on the lips.

"What do you want from me?" I demanded, out of frustration mostly, which surprised even me.

"Why I just want to be your friend," Sherry replied, smiling nervously as she pulled back away from my face.

"Then, I'm willing to be your friend when you are willing to have an authentic relationship with me," I replied with more than a hint of anger in my voice. On this point, I was clear.

Sherry was taken aback and offered no response. She went over to the other side of the room and found a chair, putting a lot of space between us. She never bothered me again. As a matter of fact, before the week's end, she had a medical emergency and had to leave the monastery returning home prematurely. I wondered, "Does she even know how to have an authentic relationship? Is there a correlation between my confrontation with her and her medical problems?"

The lecture content left me unfulfilled. The emphasis on speaking in tongues and merely token references to about 3 or 4 other gifts portrayed a bias toward the outward manifestation of spiritual gifts than inward movements of the spirit. Therefore, at lunch I found the food and company much more satisfying than the lectures. I sat with Father Coleman, who was alone over in the corner.

"Good afternoon," I said, putting my tray on the table and pulling out a chair. "Mind if I join you?"

"Afternoon, please join me," Father Coleman said, without lifting his head from the food.

"I was hoping you would share your thoughts about social justice," I reminded him, realizing we would get more talk if I gave him a topic. Also, I was aware that the class had been kicking around this topic quite a bit about the politics of gay and lesbian relationships.

As I began my meal, Father Coleman was finishing his, so it was a natural transition for him to begin talking. "Do you like bananas?" he asked.

"Yes, very much," I told him. "They're a good source of potassium. Eat them at least once a week."

"Well, my theory of social justice relates to this. The way I see it, if you consume bananas, sold by the rich people in South America who exploit the poor people doing all the work, then you should provide charity directly to the banana laborers in that country."

"Novel idea," I told him. "Simple, also," I thought to myself.

We moved on to apply the principle to other products and test it out. The simplicity appealed to me. Its universal application also proved attractive. In many ways, it was non-political and by-passed the administrative surcharges of many organized charities. This concept came to be one of the most valued gifts I received from the entire experience. I brought it home and shared it with my wife, Cecelia, who resonated with it so much that she applied it to her career. We also immediately changed the way we distributed our charitable contributions, making that spiritual discipline of our more in alignment with this theory of social justice. My future self probably saw its value in greater depth than other parts of me. The evidence is that it has endured the passing of time. So, Father Coleman, I officially give you a belated, "Thanks."

After lunch, I had spiritual direction with Father Sam. We are getting along well.

"What do you wish to address today," Father Sam said after joining hands with me and opening with prayer.

"Since I've been here, I've had a couple of prison-related dreams. I've had them on and off since I left employment at the prison, some 14 years ago."

"I see a lot of parallels between prison life and monastic life. They're both institutions run by a patriarchal figure. They both bring a dysfunctional organizational structure by nature of the people who bring their dysfunction into the place. In some ways, they both provide a sense of safety and predictability, from the daily order of business to providing food and shelter."

"I see," Father Sam said thoughtfully. "But the major difference is that one is dedicated to receiving everyone as if they were Christ himself, while the other is based upon predatory treatment of one another. Remember the demons hang out around monasteries in greater numbers than the marketplace. I'd bet it's even fewer at prisons."

"Oh, yeah, I get it," I said, letting him know we were both on the same wave- length and somewhat impressed with his insight into prison life. "Like the prison culture, this place applies pressure for people to do things, like participate in the readings, defining what to read, hurry up from one event to another, wait until someone tells you to begin, reinforce behaviors considered positive and discourage negative behaviors. In many ways, it's like high school all over again, with people vying for popularity around here."

"Yes, it's even more observable when we invite people here for the spiritual direction schools. It's less obvious within the ranks of our residents," Father Sam added, knowing he was providing a private insight.

In that moment, only my future self would know how many of the elements of monasticism are imposed naturally on elderly people through the effects of aging and institutionalization.

Father Sam brought me back to the present advising, "The recurring nature of the dream suggests there is a message for you from God that you have yet to get. Stay with the dream and pray for the meaning to be revealed," he added.

Looking back, I wonder why he didn't educate me on the relationship between dreams and demonic possession.

"I wonder if the dream and the anger is related to Sherry and Sharon," I ventured, explaining how they had surfaced as thorns in my side so early after arriving.

"Remember, since you cannot do good to all, you are to pay special attention to those who, by the accidents of time, or place, or circumstance, are brought into closer connection with you," he replied.

I flashed to the time I was approached by a woman in Walmart weeks before Christmas asking, "Can you help me out with a few dollars?" Confusion was the dominant inner experience. I wished I had handled it better.

I had brushed her off by saying, "Lady I don't know you and I usually give to organized charities."

"Okay, Father," I added, unaware of how addressing him in this way kept us from having an equal relationship. It was more parent/child in nature.

With this last comment, we ended the session with a prayer and arranged to meet again the next week.

The next item of the day was an open invitation from Jackie, an Episcopalian priest in our class, to participate in communion, called the Eucharist by both Catholics and Episcopalians. Everyone was invited, regardless of faith background. Of course, I attended because of the openness of the invite. For me, participation in this presented no inner conflict of beliefs. The experience pulled together many of the outliers in our class and helped cement the group. If there was anyone still excluded, it probably was of their own doing, like the cigarette-smoking group who hung out on the parking lot next to our rooms. Pam and her keeper assigned to her were among that group, along with the maintenance guy, who I came to know as 'the Abbot's boy.' On the other hand, Father Nick, an Episcopalian member of the smoker's group, did participate.

The remainder of the afternoon was spent walking down by the river with my Deer friend, Karen, looking for rocks, taking pictures, journaling, and, hearing more about her marital problems.

"I've learned that you know a lot about the Enneagram," Karen offered.

"Yeah, I've been studying at the Cenacle in Houston. Sister Lois is my teacher, a nun who teaches a whole series on the Enneagram. She is also my 'at home' spiritual director."

"I'm a 4 and my husband is a 5," Karen revealed, as the basis of understanding for her relationship problems.

"Oh," I said with a look of concern on my face, knowing how aloof a 5 can be.

"I've studied the Enneagram, also," she added. "I wish I had known more about it when I married."

"Would it have really made a difference?" I asked, as I preoccupied myself with taking pictures.

"I'd like to think so," she said, now turning her attention to snapping shots of the river and surrounding rocks.

"You were probably attracted to his intellect and he was probably attracted to your heart."

"Yes, and the sex was good at first."

"Then he began treating it like sex was too much of a sacrifice, giving too much of himself, as the novelty of it all wore off," I added half as a statement and half questioning.

"Yeah, there's certainly not much of that anymore." Then added, "he doesn't want to offer a finger for fear that his entire hand will be asked for…." as if quoting somebody else.

"Okay," I'm thinking to myself. "What's wrong with this picture? Here's an attractive married woman with an advanced degree, wearing a big cross, only shadowed by her larger breasts, telling me she's not getting enough sex. She's sought me out to show me around the place. I'm the student and she's the teacher, volunteer as it may be. What's wrong with this picture?"

"Probably just wanting some free therapy," I thought as I dismissed the other possibility. So, I played along, deliberately diverting my attention to photography and studying the rocks as I walked ahead along the river. When I'm engaged in doing therapy, I am usually focused, and I deliberately control for distractions. So, one way I ensure I'm not working is to divide my attention. The other way is to return disclosure back, to keep it even. "If someone isn't interested in hearing about my stuff, then, they're just extracting free therapy," the judgmental, hurt and angry part of me thought. Like a cork, bobbling on the surface, there was no indication that the inner self was taking the bait.

So as the sun drifted toward the horizon down river, we began to work our way back to the monastery in time for the evening meal. My Deer friend seemed careful to keep herself at an arm's length when back around others. "Maybe, she's being discreet," I'm wondering, feeling a bit confused. "But, why?"

With Sherry giving me space, the rest of the covey seem to be following suit. I can only imagine how she embellished my confrontation. It wouldn't need much embellishment. I was simple and direct. Maybe her story put a bit of fear in them. Just enough to create some space. My future self knew only too well how good I am at creating space for myself.

So, I'm having a rare meal at a table with the guys, Sammy, Dave, and Rich. After finishing the meal, I moved over and had my desert with Father Lo, Father Nick, the Episcopalian priest, and Father Coleman. I asked Father Coleman to repeat his theory of social justice to Fas. Lo and Nick, who were non-conventional thinkers themselves. After desert, we moved outside to smoke and continued the discussion.

Nick, a regular member of the smoking group and apparent associate of Pam, offered, "I'm from North Carolina where we grow a fair amount of tobacco, so I do my part to support the industry." Nick dressed most days in his traditional collar and black shirt and pants.

Father Lo, who seldom dressed like a priest, said, "I'm just an occasional cigar smoker, and inexpensive ones at that."

"I like a good, expensive cigar occasionally, but they have to be pretty mild," I added while I lit up my one remaining Cohiba.

Father Coleman, dressed in his work clothes of the day, had stayed with us to further expand on the conversation about social justice. He apparently didn't smoke and offered no explanation.

"I've protested the government of El Salvador and their military practices," Lorenzo said. "They put me in prison over it. I believe you have to practice what you preach, wherever it takes you."

"I used to work in the Texas prisons, as a psychologist."

"How long?" Lorenzo asked.

"Eight years."

"I did 5 years in Joliet."

I shook my head, acknowledging I knew the place and for the others, I asked, "That was a federal prison, wasn't it?"

"Yeah."

"I was an investment banker before I became a priest in the Episcopalian church," Nick chimed in. Our church split and became a charismatic congregation."

"We've all had enough stress in our vocations to make you want to smoke," I said summing it up as I took another drag on my cigar."

"So, let's try this idea of social justice on tobacco," I offered, pulling the present moment into our conversation. "If I buy cigars from corporations, like Altria, who get rich exploiting the farmers in North Carolina or Nicaragua, how would that play out in Father Coleman's theory of justice?"

"Serve the poor people of Nicaragua," Father Lo said quickly, still holding a cigar in his mouth.

"Keeping your mission focus locally, like in North Carolina, and supporting the farmer workers' union," Nick added, with his deep, somewhat raspy voice.

Father Coleman said, "Good. I think you guys have the idea," as he walked away without saying 'good night.'

With that, the conversation was over. Everyone but me had finished their smokes, so I cut off the burned end and put it back in the metal tube it came in, stuck it in my pocket and carried it back to the room.

Dave was already in bed when I entered the room. He said I smelled of cigar smoke, so I shared with him our conversation over smokes. As usual, we shared our insights about each of those guys in Enneagram terms as we drifted off to sleep.

About 3 am, I was awakened with thoughts about the emphasis on speaking in tongues. "Did Christ speak in tongues," I wondered. What do the scriptures say? Father Andrew had pointed out the importance of reading scriptures. And he had said the gift of prophecy was more important than speaking in tongues. Further, he said it's common for one person to have the gift of speaking in tongues while another is gifted with the ability to interpret. He had also cautioned us about the danger of ego involvement in the entire process. The pressure in this group is subtle, but they seem to believe that possessing the gift of speaking in tongues is evidence that you have the Holy Spirit within you. As of yet, no one has asked me to share my faith journey and the workings of the Holy Spirit in my life. We are being taught to meet our directees where they are, but my classmates do not seem to be attempting to even find out where I am, let alone meet me there!

These were my middle of the night ponderings as I drifted back to sleep. Wednesday is another day off. I'm awakened by Dave rattling around in the room and with my night-time ponderings still on my mind, I ask him, "Have you ever wondered if Christ spoke in tongues?"

"What?" Dave asked, thrown off a bit by this question coming at him out of the blue at this early hour. He was polite in not mentioning that I had already asked him this question.

"You know, this whole speaking in tongues thing has been on my mind. I was awake for about an hour last night pondering on this. Have you ever wondered if Christ spoke in tongues?"

"Not really," Dave replied, after tuning into my thought process. "You know the Catholic Church forms faithful parishioners, not inquiring minds."

"Roomie, you're one of the most mature Catholics I know. You have an inquiring mind, especially when it comes to the Enneagram. I'm surprised you've never really pondered that question."

Repeating some of Father Andrew's lecture content, Dave instructed me again, saying, "Speaking in tongues, as a spiritual gift, usually accompanies interpretation by someone else. The prayer tongue is an acquired sound that is very specific to the individual. Prayer tongues are acquired by the ego, if you will, while the speaking and interpreting of tongues are given by the Holy Spirit. The prayer tongue is a way of ending your prayer, to fill in the 'unexpressed' things prayed for. It's willed and acknowledges the movement of the Holy Spirit and its wisdom in seeking what the soul desires, not just the ego."

"Okay, thanks for the reminder. It just seems like everyone values tongue speaking above all other gifts of the spirit," I said not realizing that I was obsessing over the subject.

"Yeah, it's part of the charismatic culture," Dave said, as if he was dismissing the subject.

"I like the sound, like a bunch of bees or the fluttering of wings, even though it comes across as just mumbling," I continued, as I pondered within my mind. "I'd like to have a scriptural reference for this," I added out loud. Then, to myself, "Is this the jealous part of me wanting to have my own special prayer tongue? Or the competitive part?"

Dave was out of the door before I finished showering, and my mind turned to food. I'm thinking about making breakfast at the first place entering Santa Fe, a roadhouse bar and grill with good food. With a day to myself, I spent the rest of the day exploring the city, shopping, getting a massage, eating out, and looking through music and bookstores.

The distance and alone time allows more pondering, "There are a lot of people here going through emotionally tough times. My role is not defined. So, I'm just staying open to the promptings of the Holy Spirit, practicing loving them, and surrendering." With a little bit of self-care, I am feeling good the last few days. "I wonder if it's due to getting Sherry off my back?" And then, "Maybe I felt more pressure from her than I admitted."

A busy day for me left me feeling very tired upon my return to the monastery. I wandered over to the Library to check email since the place seemed deserted. While checking email, the entire monastic community swarmed into the room all dressed in their formal robes worn in church services and collectively began praying out loud, apparently unaware of my presence.

By the time I had tuned in to what they were saying, I heard, "We rebuke any curses, hexes, or spells sent against us and send them directly to Jesus for Him to deal with as He will. Lord, we ask you to bless our enemies by sending your Holy Spirit to lead them and us to repentance." They went on praying this unusual prayer as I lowered my head, focusing more on what they were saying and ignoring the computer screen. "…we claim the protection of the shed blood of Jesus Christ over the demons. Thank you for your protection, Lord. Amen."

Later, I came to know this type of prayer as deliverance prayers or praying for protection. Prepared scripts were included as part of the course handouts.

Back in my room continuing to be focused on re-charging my internal battery, I pondered on the meaning of what I witnessed. Obviously, they didn't expect me to witness. It seemed like a 'behind the scenes' operation. By the time Dave arrived, it was a bit after sundown. I was reading in my recent book, as he entered.

"How was your day?" he asked, with a smile on his face.

"Great!" I replied, using a response and inflection my wife had coined and canned (in my opinion).

"What did you do?" Dave asked, as follow-up without giving it much thought.

"I got a good breakfast at the I-25 Diner and wandered on into town, making stops at the bookstores, tee shirt shops, and then hung around the Plaza all afternoon. Oh, yeah, I bought some bleach to clean the shower. You?"

"I played 18 holes of golf with Karen, the one you call High Pockets."

"Really? How did you arrange that?"

"We were just making small talk at break yesterday and the subject of golf came up. It turns out that she plays too, so we agreed to play the course in Santa Fe together today."

"That really surprises me," I admitted. "I thought she was a lesbian, or in a committed relationship because she didn't seem interested in reaching out to anybody else that much."

"Yeah," Dave admitted sheepishly, "I was wondering too, but the topic of sexuality never really came up."

"Well, she is the best looking and most intelligent unmarried woman in our class and still of child bearing age."

"Yeah, Sarah may be an adult, but so obviously immature that she has become the child in our class with many of the older women parenting her," Dave added.

Then without announcing he was switching topics, Dave asked me, "Have you ever heard of spark types, regarding the Enneagram?"

"No, that's a new one for me," I said, as I straightened up from the bed and leaned over toward him.

"I attended a workshop in Seattle once where the speaker brought it up. Never heard of it since or found it written in any of the Enneagram books."

"Tell me what it means," I continued, now giving him my undivided attention.

"Well, it seems that as you go around the Enneagram, add 4 to your type and that type is your spark type, meaning that you get along with them instantly. It's like an instant attraction, not necessarily sexual, but you just seem to get on a positive vibe with them. For example, as a one on the Enneagram, your spark type would be a 5. As a 6 on the Enneagram, my spark type would be a 1."

"Oh, so someone like Father Coleman would be my spark type."

"Yeah, and someone like you would be my spark type."

"Interesting," I added, going into so much thought about the meaning of spark types from my perspective, that I missed his reference to me being his spark type.

"I seem to get along well with 4's. I like them, and they seem to like me, like either Karen, the Deer, or the one I call High Pockets."

Dave confirmed his agreement by shaking his head, and adding, "Yeah, I think they are both 4's as are many women who show up here."

"But, if you follow the theory of spark types, fours are attracted to 8's," I argued, testing the application of Dave's insight to people we know in the class.

"First, there's not many men here," Dave argued politely. "How many of them are 8's?"

"Besides Father Sam, I'm not sure if there's another."

"My point exactly," Dave said with authority. My future self might have added Father Nick, the Episcopalian priest, but I hadn't gotten to know him so well yet.

So here we were, roommates sharing our insights on a common interest. Dave, the loyal trooper, a good Catholic boy had just spent the day golfing with the best-looking woman in our class. When he admitted it, guilt seemed to win over pride or competition and he upped his most cherished bit of Enneagram information as a result. Meanwhile, this perfectionist, in my single-minded interest in myself and the Enneagram, completely missed a veiled compliment in his assessment on why we got along so well.

No chance for me to bring up the unusual prayers I witnessed in the library, so I dismissed it. I was still pondering on Dave's outing with Karen with a smile as I entered the silence of sleep.

The day began lighting up before any sign of the sun cresting over the Eastern bluffs, with me awakening to find Dave already gone for the day. "Good," I thought to myself. "Time and space for lollygagging." I cleaned the shower with bleach while showering.

Consciously, I was just cleaning the shower. Subconsciously, I may have been doing a cleansing ceremony on the room, freeing it from negative spirits. The smell of bleach was so strong, I opened all the windows to let the room air out. So, I missed Lauds and made breakfast just in time before class began.

This morning we heard Father Andrew speak on the story of The Exodus as a metaphor for how people journey along the spiritual path. Using scriptures and a rough map, he traced God's people from slavery through salvation, receiving the covenant, being tested, and finally, the passage into the Promised Land. I could see how much of my adult life had been spent in the wilderness, both wandering and in being tested.

It has become customary to have a break after lunch, followed by a mid-afternoon event. So, I have been intentional about spending this time alone. The room still reeked of bleach smells, so I sought refuge outside. I have found a comfortable spot on the western hillside that is covered with pine and juniper needles and isolated. Shielded from the mid-day winds and spotted with shaded sun-rays, I can nap, ponder, read, journal, or just be with nature.

Today I chose to listen to my book on CD, *The Power of Now*. Tolle, the author, has a hypnotic effect on me anyway. Soon I find myself delving deeply into the NOW, snoring occasionally as I sleep. Upon awakening, I gave a bit of a start, unsure of how long I had been sleeping, and hurried back to my process group which was due to begin at 3 o'clock. I had ten minutes to spare when I found our meeting room back at the monastery building.

Process group, sharing group, call it what you want. It was a way for people to pose individual questions that our large class had no time to handle. So today we focused on how to deal with specific situations in spiritual direction relationships. I found myself offering ideas, techniques, and methods of handling problem situations. I had been challenged to share by Sharon, so I figured I had lots to share in these situations with my prior experience as a therapist.

Afterwards, I had spiritual direction with Father Sam. As usual, he modeled how to begin a spiritual direction session by grasping my hands and praying. We mostly visited with each other, shared life experiences, while he gently addressed the idea of peace and forgiveness in lieu of carrying a grudge and/or getting even. "I think he enjoys our time together as much as I do," I think to myself. "This is what spiritual direction is," I find myself thinking, "like the title of Morton Kelsey's spiritual direction book: Spiritual Companions."

My plan tonight is the same as last night: sequester myself in the room and journal or read. So, after the evening meal, I made a beeline to the room and locked the door. The smell of bleach had diminished since I left the windows open all day. I was happy to have a clean shower void of other people's germs.

Around dark God provided me another interruption. Bill and Martha, our dance instructors who had publicly witnessed to our class how God had healed their relationship, were standing at my door. They came, asking me for healing prayer. What followed made me believe that this request wasn't altogether honest, since they had obviously not discussed the specifics with each other.

To my surprise, Martha began describing their sex life, complaining that he no longer seemed interested in her sexually. She went on to say that with the waning of interest in sex had gone the frequency of physical touch, hugging and cuddling, and the kisses. Bill was clearly caught off guard, freezing up in the face of this exposure of intimate details in their relationship.

From my perspective, here was a late 60's, early 70's couple who seemed to have enjoyed some physical attractiveness in their younger days. Even as they had aged, they were still very graceful and energetic as a dancing couple. I had made a connection with Bill but was not at all interested in their sex life. Feeling somewhat ambushed and imposed upon, I had no other instinct than to give her what she wanted: prayer for healing.

So, I avoided questioning about the issue – I was not
interested in any more details. I offered no 'patient education,'
wanting to be clear that I was not participating in this as a
psychologist, but as a lay-person. I did ask them to kneel with me
around my little bed, holding hands, while I prayed in earnest to
God, the Son, and the Holy Spirit for healing of their marriage
relationship. It was completely dark outside when they finally left.
I had no sense of the passing of time, just the immediacy of the
situation. I could still feel the heat of Bill's embarrassment after
they exited the room and could feel a smoldering resentment
building within me toward her. "Does she still think of herself as
sexually attractive?" I wondered. "Clues into the nature of their
marital problems," I thought to myself and then, "Where is my
roommate when I need him?"

"Is this what Charismatic Catholics do in community?" I
asked myself. "For people who put so much faith in healing by the
Holy Spirit, they seem to have a parallel faith in psychology."

Dave must have quietly entered the room and gone directly to
bed because I remembered no sound of his coming.  My morning
thoughts centered around what I considered to be a gross boundary
that was crossed last night by them and a general lack of
consideration for everyone by Martha. I wasn't that fond of
Martha. Maybe she reminded me too much of Sherry (who
reminded me of my ex-wife), a bit too superficial and more
concerned with her agenda than the impact on others. Either way, I
would talk with Dave and Sammy about it later. "No time now," I
thought, "it's time for a silent breakfast."

The lecture this morning focused on healing the family tree.
To guide the process of identifying areas in need of healing, the
genogram was introduced. A genogram is a family tree that
includes a medical/emotional health history, as well as relationship
patterns and roles played by members. While I use genograms in
my work and like what they usually yield, the lecture offered a
much deeper approach along with specific prayers to use in certain
situations. It was announced that the next day our class will have

another healing mass specifically for healing the family tree, and the genogram information will be preparation for that. We were asked to prepare prayers for deceased loved ones that would be used during the healing Mass. You can go as far up the family tree as desired. To this Methodist, the assignment seemed to have a very Catholic perspective.

By mid-afternoon, it was time for our last dance class. I arrived early and found Bill alone in the classroom reading his Bible. "I was a bit embarrassed by the topics you guys brought to me for help with last night," I started out.

"Wait a minute," Bill quickly said. "I was just as surprised and embarrassed as you were. I thought we were just dropping by to ask for a general blessing of our ministry and the marriage relationship that makes it possible."

"Sorry, I know you were embarrassed. Want to talk about it?"

"Not really, I haven't sorted out all my feelings yet," Bill said as he turned back to his Bible.

Having arrived to class early to have that conversation, and it being cut short, I had nothing left to do but go to the other side of the room and make notes in my journal, pray, and ponder what just happened.

By the time everyone else arrived and we were ready for class to begin, Bill seemed to have gathered himself and be okay. We never talked about it further. This was the third class of their series. They left that afternoon and I never saw them or heard from them again. His wife seemed bound up in lots of drama and manipulation. Her sense of ministry seemed to reinforce this in some weird way. "There's a fine line between ministry and manipulation," I concluded as I filed them away in my expanding vault of confidential memories of other people's issues. If I had a clinical supervisor, she would have reminded me that they weren't my clients, she crossed my boundaries, and there was never any promise of confidentiality between us. But, I was in the habit of filing away confidential information in my vault.

I felt so much empathy for Bill. "If there ever was a time for healing to happen in a relationship, it occurred to me, "this is it. What happens between them impacts an entire ministry! The benefits multiply exponentially as do the costs."

Sad. All this healing of the family tree, inner child work through dance, and insight into the nature of Bill's marriage leaves me feeling sad. "Or is it grief?" I ask myself. "Lord knows I've had enough grief in my life." Either way my mood was taking a downswing.

The evening meal was more noticeably even more meager tonight. There must be something about a Friday night in the Catholic week that leaves the cupboard bare. Was this a 'no meat on Friday' fast? Or low on funds?

After dinner, a group of us gathered in the coffee room and spontaneously agreed to make a trip to the local Dairy Queen for dessert. Originally, it was me, Zoe, Jackie and Susan.

The ride there gave us just enough time to get better acquainted. We learned that Zoe, has previously worked at several seminaries as a teacher, helped put on retreats and seminars herself and follows where the Holy Spirit leads, with her husband serving the Lord. Jackie, an Episcopalian priest from Hawaii, who has formerly served in the military as a chaplain is questioning her sexual orientation, even though she is married. Susan, whom I had nicknamed Suzie and had the emergency with her eye, is about to graduate from seminary and is going through a divorce. And Will? Hey, maybe Sharon's accusation of me not sharing enough is right. "Maybe I'm NOT open enough," I wondered for the first time.

By the time we arrived, we found that much of the class was already there, in line to order ice cream. The immersion in course materials and the emotional impact of the experiences must have been building up in everyone. "Relief-seeking behavior," I thought. The trip provided just that, a temporary pleasure that distracted and provided an escape from the seriousness of the day.

While there, I took an opportunity to talk with Sarah, the adopted child in class, about vocational choices in relation to the Myers-Briggs results. We ended up talking about her trust issues and loneliness. I gave her some practical suggestions about building trust in relationships. She impressed me as an emotionally immature 23-year-old who may have been materially indulged and emotionally neglected by her parents. Also, she seemed devoid of certain social skills we take for granted. "Yeah, I'm a quick study," I thought inwardly as I drove back to our home away from home. . ..

Awakened by another dream, I slipped out of bed and walked quietly to the break room to journal. I wasn't surprised to find Alisa there. After journaling my thoughts, I bypassed coffee and visited briefly with Alisa before returning to bed. "Comfortable," I said to myself as I walked back to the room thinking about Alisa.

Saturday begins like most other days. I'm beginning to feel comfortable with the routine. "How quickly we become institutionalized," I thought. Roomie had already left for the morning, and I had plenty of time to reflect on the activities of the previous evening, as I prepare for the day.

Coffee and breakfast in silence. I could get used to this part of monastic life. "Maybe I was a monk in a previous life," I pondered. A part of me toys with the idea of past lives. The scripture doesn't address the concept directly, but does make some indirect references in the gospels. For example, when Christ asks his disciples, "Who do people say I am?" They reply, "Some say John the Baptist, others say Elijah; and still others, Jeremiah or one of the prophets." My hooded sweatshirt adds to the image when I walk around in the cold in my hooded sweatshirt with my head covered, carrying my walking stick it does add to the image. I do relate to the masculine energy of the prophet, John, the Baptist.

Today we hear Sister Hillary speak about St. Gregory and his insights into Christian mysticism and Father Andrew, teaching on the initiation into adulthood, using Christ's life as revealed in the scriptures, He draws specifically on the stories of Christ's baptism, temptation, and the beginnings of His ministry relating them to our adult life experiences. Both lectures were splendid.

As I can remain focused on the present moment, the 'Now,' as I have learned to call it, I find myself paying more attention to the relationships I am developing, than to the lecture content. I ponder more over the people I'm interacting with than the material I'm learning. "Not sure what this means, just going with the flow," the analyst in me concluded.

This afternoon was highlighted by the class-sponsored mass dedicated to Healing the Family Tree that we were introduced to and worked with yesterday. It was led by Father Sam, who offered prayers over our family trees and ancestral sins. It is a relatively simple ritual that ends with taking communion and receiving the anointing with oil. Each class member provided a list of family names that were deposited in a prayer basket, prayed over and, finally, burned collectively in the fireplace along with incense. The symbolic intent was to raise the concerns to the Heavens and let them go in faith, anticipating a healing for the class and their issues.

After the ceremonies were over, Father Lorenzo, Sammy, and Zoe accompanied me to Pecos for a Mexican dinner and a beer. Father Lo shared more about his missionary travels in South America and his work as a social activist speaking and acting in opposition to US policies involving South American governments.

Father Lo, "Yeah, I was arrested several times in the States and even went to prison."

"What happened?" Zoe asked.

"I was with a group protesting training of El Salvadoran troops by the US military. We interrupted their training and sleep by posting loud speakers around their training camp at odd times. We were arrested by the military police, tried in Federal court and sent to a Federal prison," Father Lo said, giving a hint that he was in storytelling mode as his eyes lit up.

"What other prisons did you do time in?" I asked, hinting that he and I had already talked about this before.

"Kentucky and Illinois state prison."

"Oh, yeah. I worked briefly in a Kentucky federal prison while I was an army physician," Sammy offered finding a way to interject himself into the story.

"Strange," Zoe said, reflectively, "I did volunteer ministries in prisons and was in that same prison in Kentucky."

"What year were you there?" I asked, looking directly at her.

"1985."

Turning and looking at Sammy, I asked him the same question.

"During the late '60's. Vietnam era."

"How about you?" Looking at Father Lo.

"Let's see, it was during the civil war time in El Salvador. It lasted a long time. Must've been the '80's, late 80's, around the time those Jesuit priests and their housekeeper were murdered, and we were training the Salvadoran military in the US."

"All of us working in a prison. The three of you working for God brought you to the same prison at different times from different perspectives. What are the odds of that?" I asked out loud, but more like I was talking to myself.

Father Lo continued to talk about the politics of those days, the Carter administration and how the Regan administration switched tactics with El Salvador. He was experienced with 'liberation theology,' a prevailing mission theme during the '80's.

I wondered if Sammy or Zoe were thinking what I was, "This guy, Father Lo, is the real deal." In my search for authenticity, I had stumbled upon one of the most authentic people I had ever known. He was living a Christ-like life, in my opinion.

"Divine synchronicity," Father Sam announced, at our next spiritual direction session when I shared this coincidence with him, reflecting his knowledge of Carl Jung's work. I had already known that the residents were well schooled in the work of Jung, the Swiss psychiatrist from reading their pamphlets and following their newsletter.

Over the course of our time together here, I had become aware of a concern among the women of our class: sexuality preferences. Somehow, they had it connected to social justice, which was currently popular among the Catholics, much like liberation theology was with many during the '80's. From my experience in leading therapy groups and teaching group counseling techniques to other professionals, I was aware of the benefits of a group being aware of … itself. I was feeling an urge to 'help' our class come to an awareness of how the issue of sexual preferences, namely homosexuality, was being bounced around between the women of the group. Some were announcing that they had discovered they were lesbian, even after years of marriage. Others were being more private about their preferences. I concluded that it was common knowledge that they were meeting separately to discuss these issues, even though the men were not included.

Self-appointed, the Sir Lancelot, questing knight part of me decided (as opposed to praying about it and seeking divine guidance) to 'help' the class become more aware of what I considered a blind spot of the group. So, I took it upon myself to invite the women of the class to an evening study group and discuss heterosexuality. My future self was the only one who understands the error of this decision. In the very act of deciding, I was killing the possibility of having a positive relationship with these women. Think: suicide, homicide, genocide, decide…. It's all about free will, the power to decide. When choices are only focused on self-preservation, we kill alternatives for relationship building.

The invitation, written on the chalkboard in the Monday lecture room read: *The women of the class are invited to room 315 at 7pm tonight for an evening of heterosexual discourse.*

As an afterthought, I told Brother Dave, my Roomie what I had planned. "It would all be over by the time he came back to the room anyway," I reasoned, "plus, he's invited."

Dave's response when I informed him, "Well (after a long pause), I don't really know you at all (emphasis on last word)."

That night, most of the men of the class showed up. I had prepared snacks to eat, pads of paper to make notes, and brought in a few extra chairs. Dave didn't show. Sister Hillary passed by the room, as if patrolling the halls. No women showed up.

Confusion was the prevailing response. Some were indifferent to the whole thing. Many wondered what the invitation meant. Some misinterpreted. I'm sure others had other preoccupations. There was a lot of talk behind my back. Few approached me for clarification.

Karen, aka, High Pockets, was one of the few to take a direct approach.

"So, what was that invitation to the gathering last night all about," Karen asked, looking back to see if anyone else was in the room.

Looking around too, making sure we could keep the conversation private, I asked her, "Can we take this to the small room next to the bookstore?"

"Yeah, sure," she replied and started walking in that direction with me following.

As we entered the small room, closed the door for privacy, and sat, I began, "You see, when I first started working in the field of mental health, we used the DSM-II."

"Today we reference the DSM-IV."

She nodded knowingly.

I continued, "Homosexuality was classified as a mental disorder. If you were homosexual, but didn't want to be, it was classified as Ego-dystonic homosexuality."

"I see."

"When the DSM-III was published, there were political activists who swayed the committee to leave out a diagnosis of homosexuality. From there, political activists have moved on to take that behavior from bad to acceptable in the three institutions of social control: mental health system, religious system, and criminal justice system. In the process, they have created another institution of social control: the media. This business of re-defining a behavior from bad to okay troubles the perfectionist in me." It offends the Old Testament scholar in me who still thinks that the old scriptures speak to us today. I wonder aloud, "What other aberrant behavior in our society has been systematically re-defined from wrong to okay?"

She thought a minute, before responding, then said, "I'm not sure."

Why I felt this need to defend is beyond me, "I was just attempting to help our class become more aware of how they were over-balanced toward homosexuality and not talking about other points of view. I was trying to initiate a dialogue, like they were having with each other, but across genders. I was attempting to help them come to a point of awareness of how they were handling the matter as a group."

Karen offered no counter-arguments, but simply stated as she got up from her chair and headed to the door, "This is probably the most honest conversation I've ever had with anyone on this subject."

I feel confident that Karen acted as a messenger to the female classmates who had been meeting and having discussions. I figured that she probably carried my explanation back to them. Mission accomplished, at least partially.

A prevailing belief, that homosexuality begins at birth, is not supported by close attention to the research. Why some people feel safer with same sex romantic relationships is beyond me, but this may be the closer to the psychological truth. In either case, I lean more toward psychological over biological causation.

A Methodist in a monastery | Billy D. Haddock

*All are welcomed as the Christ*

# 6 Re-entry

On Monday, the beginning of our last week of the school, it was announced that there would be a special meal and celebration on Saturday. In preparation for that final day at the monastery, each small group was given the assignment of creating a skit to illustrate what we had learned during the past month. Our group came up with the idea of playing Native Americans and alternately quoting our teachers, especially things we felt were unique to the individual teacher and possibly over-emphasized. We worked independently as groups without sharing our themes with the others.

Father Sam and I got together on Friday and baked oatmeal

cookies for the celebration. Apparently, he had gained permission to work in the monastery kitchen and cook in their new convection oven. Of course, we continued the banter back and forth that had evolved as part of our relationship. He seemed to enjoy that I was willing to poke fun at him and relate with more as equals than as a father to a child. To feel included in his life this small way was his humble way of honoring our relationship. It had become obvious to me that he had special permissions to do things around the monastery that may not have been available to the others. Knowing Father Sam, I found myself wondering if these 'permissions' were granted or just taken without asking.

During the cookie making, Terry sought me out to talk. I remembered that he was a deacon in his parish church and was with his wife, Carolyn, who was suffering with COPD. We had visited very little beyond initial greetings at the beginning of the month.

He spoke to me in a loud, confrontational manner, "What did you think you were doing when you invited the women to your room on Monday night?" He looked me right in the eye and squared off physically as if to attack.

"I probably didn't think the same thing you did," I said feeling myself go on the defense, but unafraid. I was more comfortable with confrontation than most people. Subconsciously, I assumed Father Sam was too.

"It (the invite) seemed a bit too personal to me," he said vehemently.

"That was not my intent. I was just trying to make a point with the group," I countered, standing my ground.

Then I gave him basically the same explanation that I had given Karen. I doubted he and Carolyn had been a part of the discussions about sexuality, so I may have blindsided him with the invitation. "We all have blind spots," I reminded myself.

Terry seemed oblivious to the fact that Father Sam was standing right there. To his credit, he did not try to draw Father Sam into it. My explanation seemed to satisfy Terry, almost as much as confronting me about it did, I imagine.

To check myself out, I discussed the whole thing with Father Sam while we waited for the cookies to bake. He didn't seem to think much about it and certainly didn't think I had offended anyone. He was probably one of the group who was preoccupied with other matters. Although I missed it at the time, my future self noticed that the more intelligent men on the scene missed the significance of my actions while the more intelligent women were curious as to what I was doing.

Meanwhile, I was preparing my own parting gift for the residents. As we neared the end of our time together, I could sense my classmates were setting their sights on the future and pulling away from each other. I took this time to reflect on my experiences there. The analyst in me decided to provide evaluative information to Father Andrew, as director of the school. In my doctoral studies, I had taken courses in both planning and evaluation. I also had experience in program evaluation, so I was equipped with know-how, experience, and innate abilities provided by my personality.

At this point, my future self could have stepped in and confronted the rest of me about making unilateral decisions. This lesson was still forming, but my future self already knew: I make decisions that are often divisive and hurtful (without checking in with God). The operative word here is 'decide,' sharing the root with homicide and suicide. However, it was only natural (read: habitual) to decide to offer evaluative information to the residents.

Knowing there was some dissension between the sisters and the monks, I addressed the excessive draw on their resources that resulted from them trying to manage taking care of one demon possessed person while running a school for spiritual directors with 30 students who had paid handsomely for the experience. The age and credentials of the instructors was addressed next. With few exceptions, they weren't staying current and were an aging group. I expressed the need for an update: in sequencing of subject matter, in credentials of speakers, in subjects covered. As a group, they needed ongoing evaluation and upgrading. 'Decay,' was the word that came to mind.

I shared these evaluative opinions with Father Andrew while we walked around the grounds outside the buildings of the monastery. He was polite and attentive, offering no defensive remarks. Who knows what was going on inside his mind or what kind of consultation he sought before even agreeing to visit with me. I considered little of this at the time.

I did not mention my frustration with volunteers and teachers coming to me with their personal problems. I guess I considered that to be between me and God, since I had been practicing surrender to those situations.

Although it was somewhat arrogant of me to offer evaluative information, this move was my effort to inform the right person of my grievances. Several of the women in our class had aired similar complaints and talked about going to the Abbot. I had suggested they go talk with Father Andrew first, then reserve the Abbot for a group talk, if needed. "It's scriptural. Matthew 18, I think," I advised them.

That final day began with people in the dining room buzzing about the angelic figure showing itself on the ridge as the sun rose above the eastern mountain across the river. People were looking out the window while this figure stood tall with arms outstretched dressed in a white robe with the rays of the morning sun spotlighting this symbol of purity. I will admit that the sight of it was both inspiring and touching. The appearance of an angel or simulation of it just added to the already present feeling that God had been among us the entire month. After some discussion, someone announced that it was Zoe. It was a dramatic sight, which forewarned us of more drama to come.

The morning had been set aside for the small groups to practice skits for the evening performance. The afternoon was free to pack and prepare for departure on Sunday. I was nervous about our skit, primarily because I had been a leader in shaping the idea. No one else had surfaced with a creative idea or seemed to want to lead, so I took charge. In preparation for the skit, I went off-campus to the local lumber-yard in Pecos to pick up some sections of one-half inch pipe joints to assemble a make-shift peace pipe. Satisfied with the results, I felt my anxiety lessening and thoughts turning to seeing my wife.

She had planned to fly to Albuquerque and meet me at the airport. She had reservations in Santa Fe at a local bed and breakfast for our reunion. She had been invited to the celebration and I arranged a time to pick her up on Saturday afternoon.

The drive to Albuquerque was uneventful. It was another sunny day. I imagined the traffic was busier than usual since it was a weekend day. On the way there I had time to reflect on the highlights of my experiences, so I could talk with her about them in more detail. We had talked briefly on the phone and exchanged cards and notes, but had limited our exchanges. I knew she had a lot of unanswered questions. This was her nature. So, I spent time reflecting on the experiences and anticipating her questions as I drove toward the airport. She had already landed and picked up her luggage when I arrived in the arrivals section.

"Sweetheart, I have missed you," she said after we had put her luggage in the truck and had exited the airport.

"Me, too," I echoed back glad to see her in person after a month's absence.

"Have you been taking your meds," she asked.

"Yep," I said dismissingly.

Not dissuaded, she continued to question me, "Did you let

anyone know about your condition? How have your moods been?"

Realizing I was going to have this conversation, I gave in and said, "I didn't tell anyone about my condition. I didn't think it was their business. My moods have been mostly up or anger-oriented. I confronted two teachers, two classmates, the women collectively in the class and the mold in the shower. I only had one down swing."

"Did you get out of hand at any time?" she asked.

I knew this was code for 'delusional' and answered her accordingly, playing her game, 'No, my roomie, Dave kept me in check pretty well. The only time I came close was on Monday."

"What happened?" she asked, with a tone that revealed an expectation of hearing about some preposterous thing I'd done.

"Well, I have to give you some background to explain the whole thing," I answered, staring ahead while we entered I-25 back toward Santa Fe. I gave some background on this sub-theme among some women classmates about homosexuality and my decision to attempt to raise the group's level of awareness. I explained my plan for doing it and the apparent results, including Terry's confrontation and Karen, High Pockets, visit with me while she listened. Afterwards, she just had a few questions.

"Did you make any sexual innuendos to any of the women?"

"No."

"Did you hit on anyone?"

"No, if anything there were one or two occasions when I wasn't sure whether I was being hit on." I went on to explain Sherry's behavior and how I got her off my back. She didn't question that much and was already somewhat aware of it. Then, I explained Karen, the Deer, and how that relationship went. She had more questions about this since it was the first time I had mentioned it. I felt good, even a bit of relief, in sharing this with her.

She has a protective nature about her when it comes to my bi-polar disorder. She neither shares the knowledge of the diagnosis with others, nor allows me to get off my treatment plan to prevent relapse episodes. I still haven't totally accepted the diagnosis yet.

Satisfied with my current mental state and self-control, she fell into silence as we journeyed back to the monastery bypassing a stop at the bed and breakfast in Santa Fe.

When we arrived, people were gathering in the dining room drinking wine and visiting. I was surprised to see alcohol served since it had been prohibited during our month-long stay. We took a small glass of wine each and began visiting. Cecelia is much more social than I am and was very comfortable relating on this level, I think of it as … superficial. I guided her around to make sure she met people I liked or had already referenced so she could associate a name and a face. Sherry had left early, but I did introduce Cecelia to the rest of the covey.

After dining on a better than average meal, we gathered downstairs in the lecture room for the celebration to continue. Rich served as master of ceremonies and took center stage as each group skit was introduced. The class and their guests sat by the side-wall adjoining the break room. The residents all sat along the wall by the outside of the building. There were about three rows of us and I was on the middle row. Seated behind me was Pam, our classmate assigned to look after her on one side, and the maintenance guy, I called 'the Abbot's boy,' meaning he had been personally recruited and given a job based on a previous relationship in Louisiana. I didn't even wonder how he was connected to the Abbot (considering the recent media attention on sexual abuse by Catholic priests) or if he was connected to Pam in some other way, but I did later.

Our group performed first and accomplished the goal of

convincing our instructors we were paying attention and provided everybody both entertainment and laughter. Two other groups performed next and the night dragged a bit. Zoe had been selected to ceremoniously wash feet silently. I looked away each time she came to pick someone because of my fungus toenails. Last thing I wanted was to display my bare feet in front of the entire group. As she performed on one person at a time, I heard an air sound behind me, like the huffing and puffing of a big, bad wolf. It sounded like a great amount of wind was being pushed around in the room. My immediate thought was, "Pam! She's having a demonic episode."

Instinctively I had the urge to go into protective mode, knowing my wife was unaware of the potential danger she was in. It happened again, louder, enough to be heard by Susan on the front row and to my right. She turned sideways and looked back at me and I looked behind me, but couldn't determine who was making those sounds. By now, the Abbots boy was standing, requesting to speak.

"May I speak?" he said, looking toward the Abbot. He stood hovering over me in my chair. It wasn't Pam as I suspected, but him. However, I was already in attack mode, struggling to manage my anger.

"Yes, but make it brief," the Abbot said.

I sat there is disbelief that the Abbot had allowed this guy to interrupt the show even though it was already past 10:30pm and we had not even gotten to the punch and cookies. Since we had by-passed the stop in Santa Fe, we had not even checked in and I was unsure about the check-in process that late.

The Abbot's boy started, "I've witnessed many healings in my life. God has revealed Himself to me mostly in Louisiana," and he continued to go on providing specifics.

I looked around in the direction of the Abbot and his residents, noticing they seemed to have retreated in prayer. The smell of alcohol was strong as he was continuing to expel air from his lungs making the huffing noise that had originally alerted me. Susan looked back again as if to say, 'Do something!'

The frustration of the past 4 weeks came to a head like a volcano erupting. I stood and interrupted him by shouting, "I would tend to believe what you're saying, if you didn't smell like a brewery! I'd appreciate it if you'd just sit down and shut up!"

The Abbot's boy then admitted, "I am an alcoholic and have had too much to drink," as he sat back down in his chair behind me.

As I expressed my anger, I could feel a familiar rush of biochemicals activating non-verbal actions that would convince anyone I was prepared to fight. It was all too familiar to me. Unaware of how Cecelia was responding, I sat back down and re-grouped.

In some weird manner, I could relate to Jonah. After trying to follow his own agenda, Jonah finally surrendered to God's will and delivered God's warning to the Ninevites only to see them repent. Adding insult to injury, God accepted their repentance and changed his mind about destroying the city. I guess we all fall into that trap from time to time: trying to predict what God is about to do next.

With that acidy confrontation, Rich hurriedly intervened as Master of ceremonies and ended the show, "This ends our ceremony. Everyone is invited to stay and have refreshments in the break room next door."

Only my future-self understood how alone I was sitting there. In the decision to act, I had cut myself off from God, my wife, and my friends. Maybe that's why I noticed the Abbot and his monks seeming to go into prayer, just before I stood. They were probably checking in with God. I have often imagined how alone Christ felt hanging on the cross in that instant he took on the sins of all sinners, present and future. In some small, but significant way, I can also relate. It had happened before.

Sister Ann quickly came to the Abbot's boy, consoling him, as if he had been injured. I gathered my wife and headed for the door. A part of me wanted to shout, "What about me?" I had felt threatened, the threat of being wounded, by a demon-possessed woman, of having my wife attacked, of being subjected to the loose talk of a drunk, and, most of all, for being put in a situation where I was the only one willing to stand up to something that was terribly wrong and inappropriate.

In that moment of frustration and confrontation, I failed to realize how I, a continual recipient of God's grace, failed to offer it to the Abbot's boy and was jealous when Sister Ann offered it to him, instead of me. I failed to recognize that I was supporting my reputation of a man who didn't suffer fools gladly, but didn't let God be the one building my reputation.

As we gathered our things, I could see Father Sam coming over. He suggested, "Stay and have a cookie," when he saw us heading for the door. In the moment, I was too angry to sense God speaking to me through those words. There was holiness in those words that I failed to realize, but their lingering impact haunted me. 'Stay and have a cookie.'

I brushed him off, mumbling the legitimate excuse about having to get back to Santa Fe to check in. We left like a couple of robbers leaving a bank. Actually, I was still activated by a combination of anger and fear. "I made an ass of myself," I concluded. I felt embarrassed. I also felt disgusted because I never like being around a drunk, and was hell bent on getting out of there. I couldn't discern if I was fueled by anger, fear, or a mild dose of mania. Either way, the desire to escape was strong and the exit was quick, curt, and void of social goodbyes.

I was done, through with all this monastery drama. So, like Jonah, I left Nineveh, angry and seeking shelter elsewhere.

My wife sat silently on the seat beside me. She was waiting for me to blow off steam, if necessary. After all, she was more interested in enjoying the reunion than the drama from the monastery.

*Crucified Christ*

# 7 a monk in the world

A year later, I returned to the monastery to complete my training as a spiritual director. It only lasted two weeks and the dynamics were completely different. I saw signs that some healing had happened with class members in the interim. Also, the monastery had replaced the Abbot. Doubts about whether I would be accepted back were erased only when I showed up and could continue. Nobody talked about it.

The lingering suggestion of Father Sam's haunted me until I came to grips about my willingness to withdraw from the group and stand alone. I was ignoring my desire to be a part of the group, a community, and often, appointed myself to make a sacrificial decision to stand up against the 'wrongs' in the group. I had to reconsider if I was willing to pay that price and be more mindful in the moment. I couldn't see past my own self-righteous judgment.

Coming to grips with my diagnosis, the bipolar disorder was an inward sign of healing for me. I came to be more accepting of the disorder, its negative effects on others, and more willing to do what I was told to manage the symptoms. The down moods were easily discerned and much less rewarding. The up moods came to me more as irritability escalating into anger other than traditional symptoms of mania. They were less dramatic, but still reinforced bad behavior and fueled a grandiose sense of rightness and strength that bordered omnipotence. In an upswing, I was more inclined to war with others, even God. So, I returned as a more enlightened, subdued and medicated version of myself.

In all, that two weeks became an un-event, it was unremarkable, except to get closure. Three people didn't return to complete the experience: Cindy, Pam, and the classmate who looked after her. Cindy may have had financial issues. The reason the other two weren't there was obvious to me and I didn't ask. So, the story ends here, except for the residual effects.

It's been ten years since that time and my future self has helped make connections between lessons and the learning opportunities stemming from the time in Pecos.

I have learned how difficult it is to find like-minded people, especially if you don't see yourself in others. The Enneagram information has helped me accomplish this, somewhat. I still forget, at times. Sister Ann was more like me than I wanted to admit. She had a better grasp on the true meaning of God's grace than me. Father Sam and I (and probably Terry, maybe Father Nick) were from the same triad that moved against a threat (attack mode). Roomie Dave was everybody's Eagle Scout and mirrored by some of my closest friends today. Susan, both Karens, and even, Sharon, were probably cut from the cloth of mystics whom I revere. Sammy, Rich, and even, Sherry, were probably threes on the Enneagram and I'm still sorting out why I prefer the male version over the female version. I love the epicurean nature of the 7 and want all my financial advisors to be like Roomie Dave. Yes, the dynamic nature of the Enneagram helps me catch myself moving around in other people's personalities. I'm still learning that my point of view is just one of 9, all created in the many faces of God.

At the monastery, we were all book people, residents and students alike. A book person knows that books find them as much as they find books. During the past 10 years, one book stands out that helped me clarify what kind of monk I am. It's available in this life, not just in a past life. The book, *A Monk in the World,* written by Wayne Teasdale provides a blueprint for living in the world as a modern-day monk. He and Randy Harris, a preaching prof at Abilene Christian University, who wrote a similar book, are my role models. It's a monk that is in the world, but not of the world who lives at the very heart of things. I do relate to the mystics of the past, who were probably 4's on the Enneagram. Like Father Lo and the questing knight in me, I want to be less contemplative and more active in righting social wrongs. I want to be accessible, instead of sequestered in a monastery. I want to be engaged in the world and free of it at the same time, unattached to greed, indifference, insensitivity, noise, confusion, pettiness, tension, disease, and irreverence. I want to stay on the road to Nineveh and engage in the calling without demanding expected results, like Jonah did. I have seen the road, but like Father Sam taught me, I tend to wobble along, zigzagging from road ditch to ditch, like the drunken Abbot's boy. Decisions are just choices. To choose freedom, I must give up building a reputation on control. If I build a life moving against threats, I will miss the chance in building it on what I'm for.

My time at the monastery was brief in the grand scheme of things. As I reflect, I did get a glimpse of monastic peace and the monastic life, as imperfect as it was. I understand that a monk, female or male, is a person dedicated to seeking God and the rule of St. Benedict serves as the order of the day for anyone questing for the Ultimate Authority. So, I identified another player on my team, the inner monk in me. My job as a coach and parent to myself is to let this part have more playing time until he reaches dominance. I have seen the road to Nineveh. It is straight and narrow with many forces pulling me into the ditch. Like Jonah, my path wobbles in a crooked manner under the influence of an ego-driven agenda. Father Sam's reassuring voice echoes in my mind, 'God writes straight with crooked lines,' along with 'stay and have a cookie.'

I did some spiritual direction with Alisa focused on discerning her call to be a minister in the church and have maintained infrequent contact with her. In our travels, I saw Zoe in Arizona while on a trip to the Grand Canyon. We visited Sammy in Alabama and rode motorcycles together on our way to the beach. Susan was our tour guide for a day when we stopped in Nova Scotia during a New England fall tour. Sister Flo hosted us at the convent during a visit to South Dakota one summer. Father Lo completed and published his memoirs, which I obtained and read. Afterwards, he returned to serve in Guatemala where the news reported later that he was murdered along with two other priests in a carjacking. The Pecos monastery kept me informed through their newsletter of changes going on there. I dropped by to see Father Sam a couple times when on vacation in New Mexico.

I have accepted that I am on a faith journey and I often wobble, like a drunken, old fool. After all, everybody's under the influence of something. Susan taught me that I don't suffer fools easily, but I seem comfortable with my own foolishness, even though I hope I outlive that reputation. Did I become infested with demons while there? It's doubtful. I probably was already infested from previous exposures.

A greater truth is that we are never safe from God, from His power, His truth, His grace or God's presence. Paradoxically, we are most safe when we stay close to God. Just where He seems most helpless, is where you find his greatest strength. Just where we least expect him, He comes most fully.

I realize that being a self-made man just makes me self-righteous. Stubborn and strong-willed, I have warred with God and continue to if I'm not mindful. Am I still serving God and his people? Yes, when I'm mindful and surrender my personal agenda to the promptings of the Holy Spirit. Do I make mistakes? Of course. We serve a God of second chances. The road to Nineveh is a road that leads to results that matter. God gives us free will, the power to decide. If you don't like your choices, then choose again. This is no easy road, but if you know and follow your true calling, people will respect that. After all, everything we do is for mixed motives. Otherwise, I just serve my ego . . . or is it the demons?

## In Memory of:

Larry Rosebaugh, OMI

He took his first vows as a member of the Missionary
Oblates of Mary Immaculate (OMI) in August 1957, and
was ordained to the priesthood in March 1963.
Rosebaugh served 10 years as a missionary in Guatemala.
He ministered to youth with AIDS, crime victims and the
impoverished elderly. Rosebaugh was murdered May 18,
2009 by masked gunmen in northern Guatemala. At the
time of the attack, Rosebaugh was in a van with four other
Oblates who were headed to a meeting in Playa Grande,
Guatemala. Another priest was wounded. While the attack
was supposedly a carjacking, the killers escaped without
taking the vehicle. On October 28, 2009, Guatemalan
police captured Pedro Choc, Miguel Xo Botzoc and
Alfredo Xo. However, after almost six months of trial, the
court of Coban found them innocent and they were set free
for purported lack of hard evidence, despite the fact that the
bullet found in Rosebaugh's corpse, according
to ballistics experts, matched one of the guns, a .22 caliber
automatic Magnum owned by Choc. (Source: Wikipedia)

Memoirs:
*To Wisdom Through Failure*, by Larry Rosebaugh, OMI,
2006, EPICA.

# *ABOUT THE AUTHOR*

Bill Haddock worked as a psychotherapist, business consultant, and author. He specialized in the treatment of addictive behaviors, organizational and group dynamics, stress management and suicide.

He holds a Ph.D. in educational psychology from Texas A&M University. A licensed professional counselor with over 30 years' experience, he worked in the Texas prisons, at a university, and in private practice. He is currently retired and living in College Station, Texas